# VOID

---

## THE IMMUNE - BOOK 2

## DAVID KAZZIE

GRUB CLUB PUBLISHING

ISBN-10: 1-7331341-5-8

ISBN-13: 978-1-7331341-5-6

❀ Created with Vellum

# DEDICATION

*As Always, For My Kids*

## ALSO BY DAVID KAZZIE

THE JACKPOT (2011)

THE IMMUNE SERIES (2015)

THE LIVING (2017)

ANOMALY (2018)

THE NOTHING MEN (2019)

# ACKNOWLEDGMENTS

To Dave Buckley, Matt Phillips, Wes Walker, Scott Weinstein, Kerry Wortzel, Rima Wiggin and others for their valuable input on early drafts of the manuscript.

To Geoffrey O'Neill and James Pickral for their insight on military matters.

To Hiba Mosrie, M.D., for her assistance with medical matters.

To Rachel at Littera Designs for her beautiful cover design work on the Four-Book Edition and Debbie at The Cover Collection for her amazing work on Unraveling, Void, Evergreen, and Citadel.

All errors are mine alone.

~

*How lonely it is going to be now on the Yellow Brick Road.*

**RAY BOLGER**
**THE SCARECROW**

~

**D**awn.

The sun spread its virgin light across the plains, covering up the darkness like a fresh coat of paint. Miles Chadwick was up early, as he usually was, sipping coffee and looking out across the eight-hundred-acre Citadel compound. He kept his office in his living quarters, on the second floor of the main building. Floor-to-wall windows looked west toward the growing fields, which would provide sustenance for their new world, the proverbial bottle for the infant society. It had been a good summer for the crops, and the land was alive, breathing, pulsing. The summer harvest was in full swing, tomatoes, cucumbers, peppers, squash, zucchini coming into the kitchens by the truckload. A pair of tractors was already out, chugging along, preparing the ground for the fall planting season.

He still found it hard to believe they'd made it. They'd executed the plan to perfection. As he did every day, he thought about the first time he'd met Leon Gruber, the German billionaire who'd made all this possible. Gruber was the majority stakeholder in the Penumbra Corporation, a multinational conglomerate with nearly 100,000 employees worldwide. Penumbra had its fingers in a number of pies, most notably transportation, energy, weapons, technology, agriculture, and pharmaceuticals. Starting when he was twenty, Gruber had built the company from the ground up and held more than ninety percent of its shares.

When Gruber approached him, Chadwick had been in Special Pathogens at the Centers for Disease Control and Prevention, passed over for promotion yet again. Gruber approached him at a Wendy's near the CDC and invited him to head up his private lab, dedicated to the study of exotic pathogens. The lab was off the books, with no government oversight to interfere with their work. As he sat there, chewing his spicy chicken sandwich, Chadwick relished the idea of telling his bosses in Special Pathogens to go fuck themselves.

The facility was top notch, the security better than he'd seen at the Centers for Disease Control. He'd never asked where or how Gruber had assembled the

Citadel's stock of pathogens, the viruses and bacteria that could lay waste to millions of people; he wasn't sure he wanted to know the answer. He worked there for six months before Gruber told him what he really wanted Chadwick to do.

It had been a good six months, the most productive in Chadwick's career. He was having dinner at Gruber's home on the lake in the northwest corner of the compound, briefing the elderly man on his work. Chadwick believed he was close to developing a vaccine for Ebola Sudan; it wasn't the deadliest of the Ebola strains, but a vaccine would constitute one of modern medicine's great achievements and would be worth billions for Gruber and Chadwick. A huge victory against the tropical viruses that kept health officials around the world awake at night and wondering when one would mutate just right, bust loose like the cartoon Tasmanian devil, and take humanity down with it.

At first, Chadwick thought it had been a hypothetical question.

*Could he fashion a virus deadly enough and communicable enough to wipe out the human race?*

Enjoying the academic nature of the conversation, Chadwick talked about the challenges inherent in such an endeavor. Balancing virulence with communicability, both of which would have to be at a level unseen in human history. Engineering it so that it wouldn't discriminate against this ethnic group or that age group. Possibly a virus that was constantly mutating so that the human immune system eventually gave out. It would be tough, Chadwick had said, but not impossible.

"So will you do it?" Gruber had asked.

At first, Miles had nearly choked on his meat, laughing. But as he wiped his lips with his napkin, he looked at Gruber and knew the man was most certainly not joking. He didn't know how he knew. He just knew.

In that moment, as the proposal hung there, pure, virginal, a Schrodinger's cat of an idea that had neither been accepted nor rejected, he expected to be filled with horror. But he hadn't been. Saying yes, joining the greatest conspiracy the world had ever known, had seemed so easy, as though he had been meant to do it.

"Yes," Chadwick had said.

"I realize what I'm asking you to do," Gruber said. "But don't think of it as me asking if you to end the world.

"Think of it as my asking you to end climate change.

"Hunger.

"Racism.

"War.

"And for Zoe," Chadwick had said softly, almost unaware that he'd said it. He was almost in a trance, picturing a world that he could control, a world stripped clean of all the evil that had cut its purity like cheap heroin.

"And all the Zoes," Gruber had said, placing his hand on Chadwick's shoulder. He hadn't even realized Gruber had gotten out of his chair, now looming above him. "It's time for the world to evolve, Miles."

Chadwick drank his scotch.

"You knew I'd say yes, didn't you?" he said to Gruber, unable to look the man in the eye.

"I couldn't afford not to know," Gruber said.

And so he had gone all in with Gruber.

*Zoe.*

Chadwick tried not to think about her because it had been better, less painful, to pack it away deep, rather than think about the meth-addled mugger who had shot his new bride Zoe, six months pregnant, right there at the ATM machine in Atlanta for the forty dollars she had just withdrawn. Twenty-eight years old, a brilliant career ahead of him, and just like that, his life had been turned into a smoking crater. Her killer had never been caught, and Miles took some small measure of comfort in the thought that the virus had almost certainly exacted justice for him and Zoe and their unborn baby. When you got right down to it, the virus had been for *him*.

So he'd worked and worked, creating iteration after iteration, each virus coming up a bit short until finally, he'd developed Medusa (although it hadn't been his name for the virus, he thought it was terribly apropos). Then the gathering of the test subjects, the runaways, the vagrants, the homeless, the ones who had already slipped through the cracks and wouldn't be missed. That last clinical trial was unlike anything he'd ever seen. Aerosol infection of Patient Zero, then exposing her to Patient One for less than *fifteen seconds*, then One to Two, a chain of exposures, and so on through Patient Forty-Four, the virus airborne and moving even before the host developed symptoms. The virus infected every single test subject, and within thirty-six hours of exposure, every single test subject was dead.

But left unchecked, the virus would be the villain of the story Gruber wanted to tell. No, their story needed a hero. And that was where James Rogers, a specialist in nanomedicine from one of Penumbra's subsidiaries, had come in. He used cutting-edge nanotechnology to build the vaccine, the yin to the virus' yang, the light to its dark. They'd been prouder of the vaccine than the virus, using technology to assert dominion over nature, these microscopic machines coded specifically to target and destroy the Medusa virus.

Telling Gruber about each project milestone, recruiting the team to the Citadel, planning the August release, which they had code-named Zero Day, it had all gone off without a hitch. Then about a year before

Zero Day, Chadwick received word that Gruber, who was rarely at the compound, had died at the age of eighty-four. Penumbra's general counsel, a man named Dave Buckley, had shown up at the compound bearing the news. He told Chadwick that Gruber's will had bequeathed his privately held fortune to the Citadel entity and left specific instructions that the project was to continue unabated with Chadwick at the helm.

Keens in Manhattan, the night they'd released the virus at Yankee Stadium. After Miles had received the telephone call from Patrick Riccards, his director of security, he'd kept on drinking, the alcohol serving as a restrictor plate for his panic. He'd polished off most of the bottle of Dalwhinnie and woke up the next morning with an exquisite hangover. That afternoon, he caught a flight to Omaha, where he'd left a car, and drove three hours to the Citadel compound. The place had been his home for more than a decade, and he had worked hard to integrate himself with the nearby town of Beatrice, Nebraska, about twenty miles to the east. He was generous with his time and his money, he appeared in town frequently. He was a big believer in the hide-in-plain-sight theory. There was never any local curiosity as to what went on in the compound because people just liked him so damn much. He threw parties, organized toy drives. There was even an annual 5K race for charity. Well, there had been, at least.

He'd waited out the plague at the compound, even dropping into town once the virus popped up in that section of the state. He saw patients in the local emergency room in the first week of the outbreak, before things had just totally collapsed. Even he had been stunned by the pathogen's virulence; he felt close to madness as the dead piled up, in the hospital and urgent care clinic near the center of town, in the churches and houses, from the trailer parks in the southern part of town to the aging Victorian mansions in the east. Although he'd heard about the massive traffic jams in some of the big cities, that hadn't happened in Beatrice because these people had had nowhere else to go. Many of them had never crossed the town limits in their entire lives, rooted to their birthplaces by poverty, family, lack of education, lack of opportunity.

There were one hundred of them at the Citadel now, the chosen ones, handpicked by Chadwick himself. It had been a long, careful process, one that had taken years. None of the men were older than forty-five; the oldest woman was thirty-six. His and Rogers' first recruit had been Charlie Gale, a psychiatrist who'd worked with NASA in screening candidates for a manned mission to Mars. Then the government had all but scrapped the space program, a decision that, as it turned out, had been one of the nails in humanity's coffin. A checkpoint on the highway to extinction. Chadwick had little use for a society that elected to stop learning, to stop exploring. The vast universe beyond the Earth's troposphere, a rich, undiscovered bed of mysteries, and mankind had said, *Nope, we're good!* Together, Rogers, Chadwick and Gale had developed the criteria for membership in the Citadel so they could identify those that would thrive in the new world they were creating. There was no room for error, none whatsoever. Each recruit had to be perfect.

Fifty men. Fifty women. They were doctors, engineers, scientists, botanists, agronomists, survivalists. Single and never married. No children. Rigorous physical examinations. No religious background or participation because the last thing he needed was for humanity's saviors to wipe each other out in a holy war six months later. Even more rigorous psychological evaluations, because these people had to hold up once they executed the plan.

And he didn't even put them through the Citadel screening process until he himself had performed his own thorough background check on each of them. He'd followed each of them for months, studied their habits, their trash, their comings and goings, read their Twitter feeds, subscribed to their public Facebook postings.

There had been hiccups, of course. One bright doctor, an epidemiologist who had looked terrific on paper, quickly figured out what the Citadel was up to.

That was as close as the project had come to being exposed, and that was when Chadwick realized how lucky he was to have Patrick Riccards as his head of security. Riccards was ex-CIA, a former covert operative who'd served in Afghanistan. Riccards had sensed a vibe from the kid, nothing more than a hunch. But he'd sniffed him out.

The coffee contained a healthy splash of Bailey's, a little habit he'd picked during the first week of the epidemic, as they'd watched their dark dream come to life. As they watched global news coverage delivered via the satellite linkup, as they'd stayed in contact with their field operatives, his heart was constantly racing, racing, and he found the morning cocktail helped throttle things down a bit. He didn't know why he was so on edge, why he'd been snapping at his senior advisers, even after it became clear they'd executed the plan flawlessly, that the virus had exceeded their wildest expectations. Based on some of the field reports, mortality from Medusa had exceeded ninety-eight percent in many areas.

And the nanovaccine had worked perfectly. This had been their greatest fear. That the vaccine would fail at the critical moment, that someone would break with the virus. But no one did. Three people had developed non-specific symptoms in the first week of the outbreak, incidents that had launched their collective testicles into their collective throats, but they hadn't become ill. One person had experienced a mild heart attack during the epidemic, revealing a previously undiagnosed heart condition, but he had recovered and was on medication.

It was all but over now, and it was time to look ahead. Time to begin the work that would carry him through the rest of his life. A quiet world, a blank canvas on which to paint his masterpiece. A new society in which the population was carefully controlled, in which the planet was given time to heal the scars inflicted upon it by the weighty load of seven billion people. But a world in which they'd have all the freedom they could ever want. A society free of crime, of fear, of hate, of partisanship, of ideology, of extremism, of wants, of hunger. They could recreate society in their image, in his image.

He was still considering his options regarding the unvaccinated survivors of the plague, the ones beyond these walls, the ones who, whether they knew it or not, whether they intended it or not, constituted the biggest threat to his grand vision. Chadwick estimated there were approximately five to seven million survivors in the United States alone. Not today, not next month, probably not even next year. But eventually, they could undo everything they had worked so hard to build. He'd put it off long enough. He had to spend some time coming up with a solution.

Five million survivors.

Taken out of context, the number was huge, overwhelming, the size of the Chinese Army, at least until about two weeks ago, but in truth, the number alone meant nothing. These survivors were scattered all over the place, virtually none of them would know each other, and many of those would go through another weeding out in the coming year, people who were in no position to survive the harsh reality without the modern conveniences they'd all come to depend on. As many as twenty-five percent of the survivors were under the age of eighteen. At least a million, possibly two million, wouldn't make it through the winter. And the North American landmass was enormous. Even before the epidemic, large swaths of the continent were unpopulated. These survivors were just pinpoints scattered across a blank canvas.

The rest of them, though, the ones Professor Darwin would be really impressed with, would become battle-hardened with time. They would adjust, evolve, possibly assemble into a threat, especially if they ever found out the truth about the Citadel. That was their greatest secret, the one that had to be guarded at all costs.

He drained his coffee and looked at his calendar. Chadwick had meetings this morning, meetings all day. There was so much to do, so much to keep track of. First up was Dr. James Rogers, who had been running tests on Citadel women in preparation for the project's second critical phase. Chadwick checked his watch and sighed. It was ten after six. He was already behind schedule. Rogers was due at six, and he was normally early to their meetings. As he waited, the day breaking clear and hot, he poured another cup of coffee, passing on the Bailey's this time.

Rogers knocked on the slightly ajar door just as Chadwick finished stirring in his sugar.

"Come!"

Rogers stepped in the room. The physician was pale, bleary-eyed, his clothes rumpled and disheveled. Highly unusual for the fastidious medical director of the Citadel. It was obvious he hadn't slept. Chadwick went in for a sip of his coffee, his eyes locked on Rogers' face, and ended up with a hefty gulp of the steaming liquid. He felt it scorch his tongue, and wasn't that just a hell of a way to kick off the day? All because he thought he'd seen something in Rogers' face.

"What is it?"

"You're going to want to sit down," Rogers said. He was a tall man, lean, his skin pale from years in the lab. He kept his fine blond hair short, close to the scalp. He was a brilliant pathologist and a pill popper who'd had his license to practice medicine indefinitely suspended.

Chadwick noticed that Rogers had not apologized for his tardiness, which just made Miles even more nervous. He felt the ligaments in his knees loosen, and he nonchalantly grabbed the edge of his desk, lest he collapse from nerves in front of one of his closest advisers.

"What? Is it the virus? Is someone sick?"

"No," Rogers said. "No, it's not that."

He was silent for a moment, picking at his lower lip. He didn't make eye contact with Chadwick, focusing instead on something on Chadwick's desk. Miles followed his gaze to the commemorative baseball on the corner. It had been signed by each member of the St. Louis Cardinals team that had won the 2006 World Series. Looking at the ball twisted something inside him, and he remembered how much he would miss baseball.

"The test results are back," Rogers said. "We've discovered an anomaly."

"What anomaly?"

"In the female subjects," Rogers said.

Annoyance tickled Chadwick like a feather; he hated it when scientists spoke so robotically. Maybe if they'd been a little more approachable, a little more human, maybe none of this would have been necessary. Shortly before the outbreak, Chadwick had read that sixty-one percent of the American population didn't "believe" in evolution. As though it were something you had to believe in. It was like saying you didn't believe that two plus two equaled four. He often wondered who was to blame for such a travesty. Had scientists done their jobs right, maybe the world wouldn't have needed this reboot, this reformatting of its hard drive.

"Jesus, what anomaly? Stop beating around the fucking bush."

Rogers folded his hands together and tapped the fist against his lips, like he didn't want to verbalize his next thought, lined up like a reluctant airplane waiting for takeoff.

Now Chadwick was pissed and scared; a ripple of heat shot up his back.

"We ran anti-mullerian hormone testing on all fifty females," Rogers said. He was still looking at the baseball. "This test checks ovarian reserve."

"I know what it does," Chadwick said sharply.

Rogers ignored him.

"The results were disconcerting."

Chadwick spread out his hands in front of him, as if to say, "And?"

"In each of them, the AMH levels were virtually zero," Rogers said, finally looking up at his boss. "We ran additional tests, FSH in particular, and the results were the same. Complete ovarian failure."

Chadwick sat down and scratched an itch on his palm. That had meant something once, that money was headed your way, right? Good fortune? Well, that was a load of shit because Dr. James Rogers had just dropped an atom bomb in the middle of the Citadel.

He felt a big, idiotic grin spreading across his face, and he felt his breath coming in ragged gasps.

"Ovarian failure," Chadwick said softly.

He thought about all the work they had done, the years of sacrifice, the careful, precise planning, and the idea that it had all been for nothing made his stomach flip.

And then, quite unnecessarily, Rogers added: "Miles, all of the women in the Citadel are infertile."

"How is that possible?" Chadwick asked. The question was partially rhetorical, as he already knew the answer. There were only two options.

Either the virus had sterilized the women.

Or the vaccine had.

FIFTEEN MINUTES LATER, Chadwick was in the main conference room with Rogers and his other three top advisers. Rogers and Patrick Riccards, the Citadel's director of security, were engaged in a heated discussion, on their feet, their faces red, like two baboons getting ready to tussle.

Margaret Baker, the director of operations, was in tears, something Chadwick immediately took note of. He wondered if he should cut her some slack. She was thirty-five and hoping to give birth to one of the first Citadel babies, and he could understand her despair.

But could he trust such an emotional hair trigger of a woman? He'd never seen the slightest hint of emotion from her, not even a wisp of regret or empathy as Medusa had incinerated the human race. You just never knew with some people.

If the virus was to blame, and every surviving woman on the planet was now infertile, then none of this mattered. This was all window dressing, a really shitty after-party, and they were just the epilogue. Another few decades, and the sun would set on the human race permanently. The Earth would go back to doing whatever it was doing before *Homo sapiens* became the dominant life form, and Chadwick didn't think mother Earth would miss them all that much.

He preferred this scenario because then it meant it wasn't the other scenario. If it wasn't the virus (and he really didn't think it was), that meant it was the vaccine that had done this. Their vaccine. He'd almost been prouder of the vaccine than he'd been of the virus. It had been the ultimate exercise of dominion. In Medusa, he'd created the ultimate weapon, a mechanism to alter all things. But in the vaccine, they'd created something even greater.

If Medusa was the devil, Miles Chadwick had been its God.

And all things served God. Even His fallen angels.

Or so he'd thought.

"Quiet," he said. "Everyone sit down."

He waited while they each found their seats. He was pleased and a little relieved that they responded so quickly. They sat like obedient schoolchildren, their faces open and scared and hopeful all at the same time.

"Up until now, everything has gone to plan," he said. "Better than we imagined. But now we've got our first crisis. Our first real crisis."

He thought of something else to say, but he wasn't sure how it would play. His pulse slowed, like a racecar throttling down, and he thought it ironic that it had taken the end of everything to make him feel like he was in control.

"And, quite possibly, our last crisis," he said casually.

He saw smiles on their faces, even a chuckle from Rogers. The tension seeped out of the room like a deflating balloon. It worked. They wanted leadership, and he was giving it to them. He was in charge.

"We need to find out if the infertility is a side effect of the vaccine," Chadwick said. "We need to bring in an unvaccinated female survivor. And we need one yesterday."

He looked at Patrick, who was already nodding his head, taking notes.

"I've got a team in mind already," he said. "We'll move out in the morning."

"What if it's not a side effect of the vaccine?" Margaret Baker asked stupidly.

Chadwick sniffed, and then let out a slow breath. He reminded himself she wasn't a physician. Rogers, who had been sitting quietly, his head down, focused on his hands, spoke first.

"Then we're all fucked," he said.

## 2

---

For months, Sarah Wells had been promising her father that she would come back to Raleigh for a visit, if she could just find the time. On the twenty-sixth of August, she fulfilled that vow. She parked the motorcycle on Eastwood Drive, there next to the mailbox, and secured the helmet on the handlebars, but she didn't dismount the chopper. She stared at the little Cape Cod she'd grown up in. All she had to see was the long grass, rippling in the light afternoon breeze, to know that her father was dead. He'd been religious about cutting the grass, twice a week in the summer, Sundays and Wednesdays, once a week during the winter.

It never crossed her mind that he'd fled when things started going south because that wasn't whom Ernie Wells had been. No, he was in there, no doubt about it, dead now like his wife, like his neighbors, like everyone else she knew. He had stayed and helped and checked on people until he got sick and died. She looked up and down the desolate street, this twisted, nightmarish version of the neighborhood she'd grown up in. Somewhere along the street, a loose shutter clocked against siding, the sound huge in the morning quiet. Next door, over at the Tiricos' house, a cat slinked along the front porch railing.

Sarah swung her left leg over the seat, slung her M4 over her shoulder and walked up to the front door; it was cracked open, and a terrible mustiness tickled her nose. She poked the door open with the muzzle of her rifle, revealing in full color what she knew to be true. There he lay in his recliner, wearing his dungarees as he called them, a white t-shirt (and she ignored the dried blood spatter) and, of course, those suspenders because he'd been a slight man, thin his whole life from his career as a mailman. A blue blanket was bunched up at his feet. On the end table, cold and flu medicines, a half-empty glass of 7-Up. She knew it was 7-Up and not water because there were few ills that Ernie Wells had believed a glass of cold 7-Up could not fix, and she felt the hot tears, stinging her lips as she thought about him sitting here at the end, alone, thinking that maybe one more glass of 7-Up would fix him up.

A horrible feeling swept over her; relief that he was

dead. Relieved that her own father was dead. And not just because he would be spared a life in this terrible new world or possibly reunited with his wife, dead two decades now. But because Sarah wouldn't have to face her father and tell him what she had done that terrible day on the Third Avenue Bridge. That she had "followed orders" and massacred civilians, that she had hurt the ones she had sworn to protect. And for what? A quarantine that was obsolete the moment it had been ordered.

It hadn't taken her long to see the folly of the mission. Across the river in a canoe, through the dead streets of Manhattan, block after disease-ravaged block. Everything outside her Q zone had been just as fucked up as it was inside their little cocoon. Her quarantine, and her God-blessed attempt to hold it, had been nothing more than window dressing, something for the bigwigs, for the deciders, to do to make them feel like they were doing something, even as everything spun out of control.

She covered her father with the blanket and went around the house, tidying up. He had been a fastidious man, and she had no idea what she was supposed to do with his body, but she could at least put the house back the way he liked it. Orderly. She cleaned for the rest of the day, until the daylight started to go, until the small of her back ached, and her hands became stiff.

For dinner, she ate some beef stew she found in the

pantry, straight from the can. It wasn't great cold, but she'd had worse on her tours of duty.

When she was done, she sat back down on the couch and dug the bottle of tetrabenazine out of her pack. She rolled the amber-colored cylinder between her hands, turning her head just so, the moonlight glinting off the bottle. There were a dozen pills left, her first go around with the medication that would merely manage the disease that would ultimately kill her.

She was such a coward.

She hadn't even been able to tell him about the diagnosis; how had she ever thought she would tell him about what had happened in the Bronx? Four years she'd been living with it, four years since she'd sat in that doctor's office in Olympia, Washington and he'd told her the bad news from behind his desk with his stupid horn-rimmed glasses, that she carried the gene for Huntington's disease. It had killed her mother, and so there was already a fifty percent chance she would get it, and wouldn't you know it, things hadn't broken her way. So here she was, staring death in the face, probably before she turned forty.

Then the plague had come, and she had prayed for death via Medusa, because that killed you quick, and she wouldn't have to suffer for years on end the way her mother had. Two days of fever and internal bleeding and coughing? That was nothing compared to what Karen Wells had endured in the last three years of her life.

But because the universe was a real bitch, I mean, a real Grade-A megabitch, she'd survived the epidemic and she wouldn't be getting an early exit after all, and Huntington's would be waiting for her like it had been all along. She'd been to Iraq and Afghanistan four times; each time, she'd made it home very little physically worse for the wear. The worst injury she'd suffered was a nick in her arm from an IED that had killed six of her fellow soldiers.

Because of course.

And back up in the Bronx, the rest of her platoon had died. She had stayed with them after the thing with the bridge, and she had watched them die, one at a time, punishment for her sins at the bridge. Then she received that bizarre final order from HQ, and when she was done here, she would carry out that order.

Because of course.

She unscrewed the cap and popped the chalky pill into her mouth, where she let it sit for a moment. She could feel it dissolving, the chalky bitterness spreading on her tongue, hitting her gums, and for a moment, she considered spitting it out, and being done with it. No more treatment, no more delaying the inevitable.

But she threw her head back, washing it down with her father's flat 7-Up. It slid down her throat just as smooth as good wine, and she cried.

## 3

I t seemed a little strange to Freddie Briggs that he was even bothering with breakfast, given what he had planned for this morning, but there you go. He couldn't remember the last time he'd skipped his morning meal, and he wasn't going to start now. His mother wouldn't have approved, and he figured he'd better do something she'd have been happy with before the day was out.

And so Freddie Briggs sat on the curb in front of the Cave Spring branch of the Rome Public Library in northwest Georgia, chewing robotically on a Pop-Tart as the day warmed and then blistered before him. He grimaced at the sickly sweet taste, wondering why they hadn't improved their formula in the last two decades. They tasted the same today as they did when he'd first started eating them as a freshman linebacker at LSU, back when he couldn't consume enough calories to keep the weight from falling off.

*Well, guess what guys, you've lost your chance!*

The library bordered a small park to the east. The smell of wet grass tickled Freddie's nose, and he was back at LSU again, back in the locker room after his very first practice. He closed his eyes as he chewed. Beyond the sweet earthiness of the practice field after a mow, the sour stench of dried sweat hung in his nostrils. The prank the seniors had played on him after that first practice, the heat so immense it felt like you were wrapped in insulation. How gullible he'd been.

"Coach wants a word," the defensive captain, an onyx-skinned cornerback, had told him.

"Really?" Briggs replied. "Coach Hyatt?"

"No, dumbass. Coach Bush. Grad assistant. Said bring your playbook."

"Playbook?"

"Did I fucking stutter?"

Freddie's tongue went numb.

*Playbook?*

So Freddie had gone looking for Coach Bush, the graduate assistant coach, who, quite frankly, Freddie couldn't even remember meeting, but that didn't mean anything to him. College football was so much bigger and faster than high school had been. He was fast and big, sure, but so was everyone. More coaches, more equipment, more plays, more everything.

And he'd met with Coach Bush, whose office was nothing more than a tiny supply closet (*gotta start somewhere*, Bush had said), and then he told Freddie he'd been cut, that they'd seen everything they needed to see about him in that first sweltering practice, that he might have been a superstar back in Smyrna, but this was Loozy-anna State, goddammit, and his game just wasn't gonna cut it in the ESS-EEE-CEE. Freddie hadn't argued with him because he worried that if he had, he'd break down in tears, and he couldn't have that.

Freddie trudged back to his locker, stepping ever so gingerly, the way a man might when he's been kicked in the nuts. He could feel the stares and he wondered if there were other freshmen meeting with other nameless, faceless graduate assistants in tiny supply closets and learning of a similar fate. They stared at him as he emptied out his locker, which still smelled like the air freshener mounted on the back, so brief had his membership on the squad been.

He made his way for the door, his gear stuffed this way and that in his equipment bag, and had his hand on the handle, the metal cold and sharp, when they burst out laughing at him. He stood there frozen, looking for the will to march out that door with his head high because they could kiss his ass, until he felt the tap on his shoulder. When he turned around, he saw "graduate assistant Coach Bush," who in reality was third-string wide receiver Ricky Bush, a senior who had never seen a single minute of action, had never even dressed for a game, and boy they had gotten him good.

Freddie lifted Bush like he was a sack of potatoes and slammed him against the wall, extinguishing the laughter like he'd yanked a plug from the wall, and he could see the sudden fear in his eyes, and that was when Briggs had known he was stronger and faster than everyone in the room.

And then he'd kissed Bush on the cheek, a loud, juicy one, and the team had roared its approval. That was the last prank he was the target of, but he'd been the engineer of many over the course of the next four years.

*Goddamn, those had been some good times.*

He wished he could keep his eyes closed forever and live it all over again, from that first game to the national championship the Tigers had won his sophomore year to the defensive player of the year award he'd won his senior year. Instead, he supposed, Coach Billy Hyatt, the AP Coach of the Year, and Ricky Bush, and all the rest were now dead.

His eyes opened, and he was back at the library again.

Ten days on the road. Ten days since he'd buried his girls, three abreast in the backyard, in Susan's flower garden, which she had loved so much. He'd tamped down the last of the dirt on Heather's grave and left Smyrna forever. He would never go home again. It was a dead place. Even Chewie, the guinea pig, had died, probably of thirst.

He had a general sense he was moving west-by-northwest, tracking the sun's path as it crossed the sky. It seemed larger and larger with each passing day, the sunsets growing ever more spectacular, exploding across the sky with oranges and reds. Maybe it was because the air was clearer now, devoid of the exhaust and smoke and pollution of a hundred million cars and smokestacks belching their byproducts into the air. Or maybe it was because of how small and alone he felt in this giant emptiness, which felt bigger with each passing minute.

At first, he'd hoped this walk he'd been on would somehow make it more bearable. That it would somehow drain away the awful reality of what had come to pass. But the pain and the grief continued to stab at him every hour, every minute, every second, like twisting, crippling arthritis.

The decision had been easier than he expected. It had left him skittish with anticipation, which, he decided, was a good sign that he'd made peace with his choice. Wherever his girls were, they were together now. And in just a few minutes, he'd be joining them. He hoped.

He finished his breakfast and, instead of leaving it

on the steps, tossed the wrapper in the metal trashcan at the base of the steps. His daughter Heather would have liked that very much. He stood up and dusted off his pants. With a fifty-foot garden hose, tightly spooled, hanging from his beefy shoulder, he crossed the tarmac toward the pickup truck that would be the instrument of his plan. The truck, a shiny red Ford F-150 he'd found abandoned near the library, was parked in a spot by the front door, its keys dangling from the ignition. He opened the door and slid in. He took a deep breath and turned the key over; the pickup's engine roared to life. In the quiet, it sounded like a jet engine.

It was a warm day, but not terribly humid, one of the nicer ones Freddie had seen since he'd left Smyrna. The sky burned a fierce blue, the sky so clear he could see the edge of it blur into the outer ridges of the troposphere. So fragile, this shell separating us from the cold vastness of space, he thought. And how fragile the world had been, far more delicate than any of them had ever thought. The shell separating them from order and chaos, life and death, creation and destruction, had been far thinner than any of them had ever imagined.

He looked up at the sky until his neck began to ache and then returned his attention to the task at hand. One end of the hose went into the Ford's tailpipe, as far as it would go, until he felt resistance.

Then he sealed off the gaps in the exhaust pipe with a length of duct tape. The other end of the hose he ran along the side of the truck, through the window, and into the driver's seat. Then he sealed up the gap left by the cracked window with more tape. A quick tug on the hose to confirm that it was well-seated in the pipe, fitted to funnel as much carbon monoxide into the truck as possible.

He felt his excitement growing, like a healthy plant getting the requisite amount of sunshine and water, fed by the fertile thoughts of extinguishing his crippling pain, of leaving behind this terrible world, of maybe, just maybe, being reunited with Susan, Caroline and Heather.

He thought he would be more afraid. But it was being here, in this world, that frightened him and chewed away at his sanity. It was a living nightmare, a twenty-four-hour-a-day hellscape that had begun the moment he'd received that first call from his daughter telling him that Susan was sick. Each successive link in the chain of events had been worse than the previous one. The panic had left him constantly shivering, as though he could never warm up.

The idea had been nagging at him, a splinter in his brain. Try as he might, he couldn't dislodge the splinter, namely because he liked the way it felt. Yeah. That was the fucked-up thing.

He liked the way it felt.

Just another fucked-up thing in a fucked-up world.

He had prayed for God to deliver him wisdom. For an answer. For a plan.

But God hadn't been there to answer. God had abandoned him in this world of the dead.

But then he had seen something that had opened that drawer in his mind, the one housing the soul's self-destruct button. He didn't think he had it in him. Oh, but he did. It was just a matter of the mind receiving the proper authentication codes, the way a submarine commander would wait for an order to launch his ICBMs. It was just a matter of God showing him what he needed to see.

Two nights ago, he'd stopped to make camp at an abandoned peach orchard in west-central Georgia, just near the state line. The sun had been low over the Great Smoky Mountains to the northwest, its rays colliding with the ever-present blue haze circling the peaks like a trendy silk scarf. As his Spaghettios heated up on the small fire, he had scoured the perimeter. Darkness was falling as he finished his sweep, a little faster than he'd expected, a reminder that he was on the back end of summer now. On the east side of the farm, he'd come across a shallow trench, muddy and sloppy on the edges. That little voice in his head had told him to turn tail and scamper back to camp. But he hadn't. He'd shone the trembling flashlight at the center of the pit.

And he so wished he hadn't.

Staring back at him in the full darkness were the lifeless eyes and pasty faces of dozens of plague victims, maybe a hundred total, all of them children. Against the harsh white light of the MagLite, the faces of the lost children floated in time and space, their paleness made ever starker by the dried blood around their noses and mouths. Babies and toddlers and school-aged kids packed together, their bodies lined up neatly. The thing that had haunted him since was that each had been lovingly set down in this mass grave, the only burial they would ever get, with some beloved childhood item tucked under an arm. A tattered Elmo doll here. A Barbie doll there. An over-sized stuffed dog, one possibly won at the county fair, curled up next to the body of an angelic-looking little girl about five years old.

He'd stumbled backwards, tripping over his own feet, dropping the flashlight. His body racked with sobs, he had fled the orchard, leaving behind his tent, his supplies, his dinner still cooking over the little fire. All night he had run as if Satan himself had crawled out of that trench. He finally had slept in a city park, with no tent and no dinner, and dreamt all night about dead children.

When he'd woken up the next morning, his body covered in dew, his mind felt sour, rotten, turned, like curdled milk. There was no sense of relief that the dream was just a dream because he knew there were shallow graves holding the bodies of dead children just like there were houses and churches and hospitals and morgues full of dead children and women and men, young and old.

That was when the idea had first came to him.

No, he wasn't afraid. This thing he was planning, that was the ticket out of all this. He didn't know or care why he'd been spared, for all the good it had done him. Susan and the girls, they'd been given a gift. Called home to God together. The punishment hadn't been dying of the plague. It had been surviving it. Left behind to make his way in this dead world, that was the punishment.

A terrifying thought gripped him.

What if God had forsaken him?

What if God had looked into Freddie's heart and decided that he wasn't worthy, and he thought back to all those times he didn't want to go to church, and, in the Great Faith Ledger of Freddie Briggs' life, he had ended up just a bit in the red.

Stop it. God forgives all. He'll forgive your sorry ass for this.

He waited as the muffler pumped the deadly gas into the car. He wanted the colorless gas to be freely flowing in the cab, filling the passenger compartment, before he got in; it would decrease the likelihood he'd chicken out before it had a chance to carry him away.

As the engine purred, he tugged on the hose to make sure it was secure.

He strolled around to the passenger side and sat down on the curb to wait. As good a time as any to pray. The church of his youth, the Smyrna Baptist Church, seemed so far away, in time and space, but it was there he looked for comfort and solace and a reminder that although what he was about to do was a sin, God would forgive him. Truth be told, he didn't think God would be all that surprised to see him.

He found himself wondering if this whole thing had been God's judgment upon man. If so, it had been a hell of a tough one. Guess we really let you down there, eh, big fella?

So this was it. He'd thought about death often, particularly during those last few minutes in the locker room on Sunday afternoons, when he'd wonder if he'd be the first NFL player to die during a game, whether he'd draw the short stick and suffer some catastrophic spinal injury and just die there on the field in front of Susan and Heather and Caroline and millions of Americans watching on television, drinking their Bud Lights and eating spicy chicken wings.

Well, football hadn't been the death of him, and neither had Medusa.

He stood up, his heart pounding, and opened the passenger-side door. The cabin exhaled a puff of warm air, the whisper of a dangerous lover. He had to act quickly, before the carbon monoxide drifted free of its enclosure and dissipated in the morning air. He stepped up on the running board, planted one foot on the floor mat and dropped his girth into the leather seat. As he leaned over to swing the door shut, entombing himself in this metal coffin for all time, he heard a noise.

This froze him. He sat there, his hand on the handle, wondering if he'd imagined it or if he was just wishing he'd imagined it.

Again — a muted, wailing sound, coming from everywhere and nowhere at the same time. A child or a woman. The sound was mournful and pathetic and beautiful at the same time, and he hated it. He wanted it to stop, he wanted it to be erased from his memory banks so he could get back to the business at hand.

Then, a voice to go with the wailing.

"Is someone there?"

Definitely a woman, the voice bearing a timbre of maturity absent from a child's. He tried to pinpoint the location of the voice, but the way acoustics had changed in the last two weeks, it could have been coming from anywhere.

"I'm hurt," the voice said. "Please. I can hear you out there."

"Dammit," he whispered, slamming a massive fist into his thigh. He held the handle tight, fully intent on slamming the door shut on that pathetic voice and this pathetic life and getting on with dying in peace. His brain had its orders, its mandate to constrict the muscles in his massive right arm authenticated. But the treasonous arm refused to budge. It would not close the door.

"Please," she said. "My name's Caroline."

Hearing his late daughter's name aloud launched him from the car like an ejector seat. Behind him, the car continued to idle, and the pent-up carbon monoxide dissipated into the atmosphere. He felt his knees go weak beneath him, and he crumpled to the ground in a puddle. The shakes were back and he felt cold, so cold.

"Where are you?" he called out, his voice booming in the morning air.

"Behind a little restaurant," Caroline called back. Her voice was everywhere, echoing against buildings, across fields and down narrow streets. "I can't move. I think my leg's broken."

"I'll find you," he said. "Just keep talking."

IT TOOK TWENTY MINUTES, but Freddie finally found the woman sitting on the stoop behind Pastrami Dan's, tucked away from the sun under a large black awning. A dozen bottles of water lay strewn at the bottom of the stairs. Her eyes were glassy, and she looked exhausted. Her long red hair was tied back in a pony-tail, revealing the fatigue in her ivory face, virtually irradiated with sunburn.

She looked about forty years old. Her light-colored blouse was matted against her torso. Her lower left leg was swollen, a dusky shade of yellow and purple. Freddie had broken enough bones in his day to know her leg was fractured. The good news was that it looked to be a simple fracture. Anything worse, she'd already be dead. But the thing that drew nearly all of Freddie's focus was the noticeable swell in the woman's belly.

Pregnant.

"Please tell me you're real," she said. "Please."

"I'm Freddie," he said, as gently as he could, unable to pull his eyes away from her very large abdomen. A pregnant woman. Until this moment, it had not occurred to him that life would, of course, at least try to go on.

"Caroline Braddock," she said. "Would you mind handing me one of those bottles?"

Freddie grabbed two, warm from the sun, and climbed the steps to the porch, where he handed them to the injured woman. She twisted off the cap and drank down the first in one swoop. After draining it, she sighed contentedly.

"Thank you," she said, the effects of the water replenishment immediately evident on her face.

"What happened?" he asked.

She nodded toward the back door of the deli.

"Found this place a couple days ago," she said, leaning her head back against the railing and twisting the cap loose from the second bottle. "It smells horrible, but there's a ton of bottled water inside. I was pretty pleased with myself, right up until the moment I tripped down these stairs here."

"Did you say this happened a couple days ago?"

She nodded. "Yeah, I've seen two sunrises."

Freddie whistled softly, trying not to think about the dark places Caroline Braddock must have gone as she sat here, crippled, unable to move, forsaken.

"I spent the first day down where you are," she continued, "but it got so hot, I pulled myself up the steps to get some shade. It's a little cooler, but not by much. I was able to carry two bottles of water up with me. That ran out last night."

She patted her belly gently. "This little guy, he's a thirsty one. Anyway, I guess I'd been asleep, and I heard your car start up or something. My lucky day, I guess."

Freddie felt shame coloring his cheeks. Here he'd been, ready to cash it all in, and this woman was fighting and clawing to stay alive. He couldn't imagine the pain she'd felt crawling up those steps, dragging her shattered leg behind her. He suddenly realized that his girls would have been profoundly disappointed in him if he'd sidled up next to them in the afterlife, not by way of the virus, but by his own hand. He felt as stupid as he'd ever felt in his entire life.

"Relax," she said, patting her belly. "I'm not having this baby today."

"I'm sorry," he said. "It just never occurred to me…"

"Well, here we are," she replied.

"When are you due?"

"About a month," she said. "Maybe less. I've kind of lost track."

"So how's that leg?"

She looked down at it.

"Fine, as long as I don't move it," she replied. "I scraped it up good coming down the steps, but I think it's healing."

"Where were you headed?" Freddie asked.

She laughed out loud.

"Headed?" she repeated. "I'm not headed anywhere. I live about ten miles from here."

"I've got a truck up the road a piece," he said. "If you'd like a ride."

Freddie felt her studying him, her green eyes cutting into him like lasers. He had a pretty good idea what she was thinking about. That it had come down to this. To putting her life in the hands of a very large man she did not know versus taking her chances here on the back stoop of Pastrami Dan's. Her whole life turned on this decision. He could see her working it out in her mind, deciding that anything would be better than dying here of thirst or starvation, or perhaps by way of a hungry animal that was getting used to the idea of the places full of rotting food, the people mysteriously absent.

At that moment, he realized how badly he wanted her to say yes, that she did want a ride. He wanted to break down in front of her and tell her that she'd be saving his life, that she already had saved his life, that he was the one owing her the gigantic favor and not the other way around.

"Where are you headed?" she asked finally.

"Honestly?" he said. He ran a hand across his scalp. "I don't know. I just want to keep moving. I need to keep moving. Maybe we can find other survivors. Maybe we can find you a doctor."

A faint smile crept across her face.

"I wish I had something better for you."

"I think I'd be more worried if you had a plan," she said.

"No," he said, thinking about the garden hose snaking its way from the tailpipe into the cabin. Oh, he'd had a plan all right. And not just any plan, but one that would almost certainly have signed Caroline's death warrant.

"I'll go get the car."

He turned to head back up the drive.

"Don't forget about me," she said, her voice quiet.

There was a sharp undercurrent of fear just below the surface of her words.

He turned back and looked her squarely in the eyes.

"No," he said as firmly as he could. "I won't forget you."

## 4

A dam woke up early on the morning of the thirtieth, the day dawning hot and steamy. Last night, exhausted, he had pitched his tent in the middle of the Duke University football field in Durham, North Carolina. He liked its clear lines of sight, which reduced the chance that someone could sneak up on him. Plus, the acoustics made for a lot of echoes, another good early-warning system. The Bermuda grass was starting to go, a little bit shaggier than you'd expect to see on a college football field, but that was true of just about everything these days.

This would be his sixth day on the road; in that time, he had only traveled about two hundred miles, far fewer than he had been hoping to log by now. But this was turning out to be no ordinary road trip, and he'd badly underestimated the impact that the world in its new state would have on him. After that last night on his couch in Richmond, he had started early on the morning of the twenty-fifth, proud of himself for his clarity of thinking. Only a fool would've started such a huge undertaking in the dark, in the middle of a storm.

As he'd driven his neighbor Jeanette's little Honda toward I-195, the local bypass feeding onto the interstate, he'd slalomed around abandoned vehicles and pileups littering the neighborhood roads. At the corner of Belmont and Main, Adam had come across the body of the cyclist he'd seen screaming past his house a few days earlier, lying face-up in the street, his ruined head propped up on the curb, as though he were using it for a pillow. His bicycle was wrapped around a telephone pole, which the cyclist apparently had struck in a last-second attempt to avoid a spilled motorcycle. The curb had cleaved the man's head open after he'd flown over the handlebars, and that had been that.

At Hamilton Street, Adam turned north and found the charred wreckage of an Army truck blocking the on-ramp to I-195, the best interstate access point for miles. Two soldiers lay dead on the ground near the truck. Adam nervously took one of their machine guns and threw it in the trunk. He had no idea how to use it, and holding it terrified him, but having it in the back of the trunk made him feel better. There was no plug of traffic here, which didn't make any sense, but he'd long since given up trying to make sense of anything.

He gave up on the interstates, figuring he'd have to follow the city streets on his way out of town.

He motored west along Grove Avenue, past quaint Cape Cods and boutique shops and trendy restaurants. The streets, littered with branches and leaves felled by the previous night's storm, were silent. No bodies here. No nothing. Then he swung north onto Granite Avenue toward a house he knew well, unable to resist the temptation; he knew he shouldn't check on his med school roommate, Mark Zalewski, and his family, but he was going to anyway. Zalewski, an oncologist, lived in a brick colonial with his wife Ashley and their three kids, two girls and a boy. Adam parked at the curb and left the engine running.

"Mark!" he called out, running up the walk. The houses around him were silent and dark, their blinds pulled tight.

The front door was open, the air rank with the hint of something sour.

"Ashley!"

He was in the foyer now, his breathing shallow and ragged. Nothing moved.

*They're dead, you know they're dead.*

But he went upstairs anyway. The boy, Parker, was at the top of the steps. He was nine years old and he lay dead in his Spider-Man pajamas. He found the girls, Scarlet and Casey, with their mother in the king-sized bed she'd shared with Mark; Ashley's arms were wrapped around her daughters, as though they'd settled in to watch a movie. Seeing them entwined in death shattered him. Mark was nowhere to be found. Knowing him, he'd gone to help at the hospital and died there. Before leaving, he carried Parker into his parents' bedroom, laid him next to his family, and covered the four of them with the comforter. Then he went back to his car and cried.

At Libbie and Grove, he saw spires of thick black smoke swirling in the early morning sky to the northwest. It reminded him of those awful images from the morning of the 9/11 terror attacks. The stink of burning char filled his nostrils; in the massive quiet, he could hear flames crackling and snapping. It looked like the fire was burning farther west, over toward the hospital. There were a few gas stations in that direction, and it wouldn't have surprised him to discover that one had gone up in flames. It was unnerving to think that this fire would burn, and it would burn, and it would burn, and no one would be coming to put it out.

The further he edged away from home, the more real it became. Everything was gone. He felt tiny, nothing more than a speck of dust fluttering through this gigantic nothingness. Nothing could've prepared him for the staggering shock of mile after mile of emptiness. Roads that were normally bustling with shoppers and delivery drivers and salespeople and stay-at-home moms were eerily quiet that Wednesday morning, August 25. Even the chaos he'd encountered coming home from Holden Beach, when mankind was still fighting, still scratching, still clawing to stay alive, was better than this.

After crossing the James River, he followed U.S. 60 east for a while, past shopping malls and car dealerships and chain restaurants and self-storage facilities. Images of a life lived here popped in his head like camera flashes. The animal shelter from which he'd adopted a lab mix puppy, dead from cancer five years now. The Korean barbecue restaurant he came to with his buddies every once in a while. Then he looped south on to Route 10 and followed it until he finally found an access point onto Interstate 85. That too, had been a difficult row to hoe, the highway peppered with traffic accidents, lanes blocked by military checkpoints in places that made no sense at all, as though the soldiers had been riding along and decided what the hell, this was as good a place as any for a checkpoint. It made Adam feel bad, that humanity hadn't been able to answer the bell, that for all its spirit, it hadn't been enough, and it was left to roll up checkpoints in rural Dinwiddie County. He averaged about forty miles a day, sleeping in his car, living off the rations he'd packed. He took frequent breaks, stopping every afternoon at two o'clock to call Rachel (unsuccessfully so far), and just trying to get his goddamn bearings. The nights were horrible, his sleep fractured by nightmares, photo negatives of all the bad dreams he'd ever had, the terror now grounded not in the fear that the dream was real but that it wasn't because nothing his dream machine had been able to conjure up had matched the broken world waiting for him each morning.

And that was how it had gone until he made it to Durham on the afternoon of the twenty-ninth, when the traffic had become overwhelming, and he'd had to abandon the vehicle at the interchange joining I-85 and U.S. 70. He packed what he could into the backpack, making sure he had Rachel's picture, and began walking. He made it to the Durham city limits as the sun began to drop, and he capped that night with a can of cold ravioli, too freaked out to even start a campfire.

He stepped out of his tent into the morning glare, needing to pee and hungry. He took care of the former need in the corner of the field, behind the end zone, and was about to address the latter when the fox struck. It snuck up on him just as he was digging through his bag for a Pop-Tart. It was a red fox, not full grown, little more than a blur that morning. Its razor sharp teeth clamped down on his wrist before he even got a clear look at it. A huge gasp of pain and shock boomed from him, and he instinctively jerked his arm around, flinging the animal loose as he scampered to his feet. It landed on its back a few feet away and then rolled back upright. Its head twitched once, twice, and then a third time. A stagger to the left before launching another attack on Adam. This time, he danced to his right, narrowly avoiding another full bite, but its teeth scraped against his leg.

Another howl of pain.

He pirouetted around to find himself looking at the fox's backside; the animal was twitching again and staring off toward the stands, as though it had forgotten what it was doing. Adam reared back and delivered a swift kick to the animal's haunches, and its rear leg snapped like a dry twig. The fox hissed and hobbled toward the sideline on three legs, keeping an eye on Adam. Then it lunged again, stumbling as it did so, its two front paws tangling together before it crashed back down. As it struggled back to its feet, Adam kicked it in the head, cracking its skull. It whimpered and went down hard. He stomped its head a second time, turning the fox's small head into a bag of broken pottery.

It was over. His legs turned to jelly, and he dropped back onto his butt. He checked his wounds; there were three raised welts on the calf of his leg where the fox's teeth had scratched him, but the skin was intact. The arm, however, was a different story. Blood seeped from the puncture wounds in his wrist and had smeared his forearm.

But the wounds themselves were the least of his concerns.

The way the fox had attacked. The bizarre twitching of its head. And how it had resumed its assault even after its leg had been broken. He clambered to his feet, dizzy. His mouth watered, but not in a good way, not in a way that suggested he was smelling a couple of ribeyes on the grill. He felt hot, very hot, like he'd spiked a fever. His dinner from the night before, meager as it was, came up all at once, in a rush; he bent over, his hands on his knees, swaying in the morning humidity. The sound of his heaves echoed off the bleachers.

His rational mind made the connection that his primal self already had.

Rabies. Rabies.

He'd just been bitten by a rabid fox.

He needed a vaccine, and he needed one now.

HE VISITED hospitals and urgent care clinics and pharmacies for three days but could not find any vaccine at all. Why that was, he did not know. Maybe in the last days of the plague, people had begun injecting themselves with anything they could find in a desperate, futile attempt to fight off Medusa. He didn't sleep, stumbling here and there looking for the only thing between him and certain awful death. At dark on the third day, he broke into a little bungalow in a quiet neighborhood on the north side of Durham. The bodies of an elderly couple were in the master bedroom, but otherwise, the house was clear, dark but for the shine of his flashlight. He found a bathroom and washed out the wound with soap and a bottle of water from the dead refrigerator.

When he was done, he sat down on the living room couch, amid the photo albums and unfinished crochet and piles of newspapers. The fear inside him was huge, even worse than when he'd been stuck with the HIV-contaminated needle. Statistically speaking, the risk from the needle stick had been extremely low, especially after the prophylactic treatment. But this. This was Medusa fear. What it must have felt like to come down with it, what it must have been to wait for the inevitable, bloody, painful end.

Now that the rabies virus was almost certainly inside him, the disease could present at any time. And once symptoms appeared, that would be it. He would die. His wrist throbbed, and he could almost hear the virus coursing through his veins. The bleeding had stopped and the wound was healing nicely, but without the vaccine, it wouldn't matter. Without the shots, sometime in the next week or next month or next year, he'd develop a cough, some numbness at the wound site, and then his brain would begin to swell and he'd develop a fear of water and then he would die a horrible, horrible death.

*This was what it was like.*

This is what it had been like for the rest of the world. As if death had wanted him all along. There was no escaping destiny, after all. That's what destiny was.

*Right on, old chap. Missed you with Medusa. Will be coming back 'round with something else for you soon.*

He was too scared to sleep.

He stayed up all night flipping through the dead couple's photo albums. He didn't know why they were out from their slot on the bookshelf; perhaps the couple had been walking down memory lane when Medusa had found this little house. They were pictures of a lifetime together, black and white wedding photographs, color pictures with that weird yellowish hue, then sweeping through the last three decades of weddings and graduations and Christmas parties and dogs and cats and fish and hamsters. Mr. Whatever-his-name-was checking out a dog on an examining table. He looked at more pictures, more and more, until he dozed and dreamed about this family and their life clicking by like a slide show, a frame at a time. As he slept, a realization flared inside his brain, exploding like a mushroom cloud, shooting him out of slumber.

The man had been a veterinarian.

Rabies.

He raced through the house, rummaging through papers and files until he found in an antique desk a business card emblazoned with the logo of the Phillips Veterinary Clinic. Mosrie Drive in Durham. He strapped on his backpack and sprinted through the dead neighborhood, following the streets out to a main artery. As dawn broke over the city, he stopped at a gas station for a map and found Mosrie Drive not a mile away.

The morning air was steamy and hot; on display around him were more scenes from the last days. Adam saw the body of a young soldier, his hands holding his rotted intestines, chewed free of his body by some heavy-caliber weapon. A black crow was perched on the man's thigh, chewing on his entrails. A turn of his head, this way or that, uncovered more visual horrors. An attractive young woman with a crowbar thrust through her neck. The head and upper torso of a middle-aged man, notably separated from his legs a few yards away. Abandoned police cruisers. A North Carolina National Guard personnel carrier. A Channel 11 news van, its satellite dish still telescoping into the sky like an alien paw. Quiet. Quiet.

The veterinary clinic was housed in a small brick building next to a Hardee's. Adam stood astride the bike, breathing hard, waiting for his heart to slow down. The terror was moon-sized now, orbiting him, threatening to fracture him. He pulled the gun from his backpack and approached the door slowly. A handwritten note on the door read *CLOSED UNTIL*

*FURTHER NOTICE*. He double-checked his flashlight and his gun. The clip was full, and he had one in the chamber.

He went inside, and the door swung shut behind him.

Weak sunbeams streamed through the large windows into the reception area, catching dust and other particulate matter floating in the ether. His heart slammed against his ribcage as though it wanted out of not just Adam's body but out of this dead place entirely. He pictured a cartoon heart scampering down the hallway, using its ventricles like legs. Maybe the rabies was already driving him insane.

He found the medication cabinet in the back, near the kennels, which were full of dead cats and dogs. He checked each kennel, one at a time, hoping that maybe there was one industrious pooch who'd hung on and could join Adam on the road. But there wasn't; there was just more death. He hoped the animals hadn't died of Medusa; it was hard to imagine a world without dogs. He rifled through bottles and vials, antibiotics and emetics and pain pills, chicken- flavored this or that, and then he found it on a shelf. A five-dose package of human rabies vaccine. A dose of immune globulin and four doses of the vaccine itself. He grabbed it along with some syringes and hustled back outside, thanking his lucky stars. It had been illegal for a vet to house or administer human rabies vaccine.

Tears filled his eyes as he read the instructions inside the shrink-wrap. He was supposed to have taken the first dose on the day of the bite, but there was nothing that could be done about that now. He injected the globulin and first dose of vaccine and prayed that he'd done it in time. The other three doses would follow in three, seven and fourteen days. All he could do was hope and pray. Pray that he wasn't left to die of perhaps the one disease even deadlier than Medusa.

The tears burst forth, and he cried, sitting there on the curb outside the Phillips Veterinary Clinic.

"Are you okay?"

The voice startled him so badly he gasped. He couldn't remember the last time he'd heard a human voice. He opened his eyes and saw an attractive young black woman wearing an urban camouflage uniform and holding a gun on him.

He stared at her, debating whether she was really there or if he was hallucinating.

"You gonna freak out on me here?" she asked.

He felt his jaw moving, but no words would come out.

"I'm going to count to ten," she said, "and then I'm going to head on down the road."

Then more quietly: "Jesus, can I not catch a break?"

"No," Adam said. "I'm fine."

"What's with the needles?" she asked. "No hospitals if you O.D."

Adam glanced down at the paraphernalia around him and smiled.

"Oh, no. It's not that. I got bitten by a rabid fox a few days ago," he said, pointing to the bite marks on his arm. "I finally found some vaccine for it."

He watched her watch him, staring at him with her fierce green eyes, as though she was trying to decide whether to believe him.

"My name is Adam."

THE DAY BRIGHTENED AROUND HIM, the morning cloud cover pushing off to the east. As they stood there in the parking lot, he felt very small, very alone.

"Adam Fisher," he said again, extending his hand.

Her eyes narrowed as she considered his offer of goodwill. His outstretched hand hung there in the void, suspended, frozen in time.

"Relax, you can't catch rabies from me."

It was just the right thing at the right time, and a smile broke across her face. It lassoed them together, keeping the quickly widening gulf between them from getting any bigger. She took his hand and returned the shake.

"Captain Sarah Wells," she replied. "U.S. Army."

They fell into a brief silence.

"Sounds silly, doesn't it?" she asked.

"What's that?"

"Captain Sarah Wells," she said again, this time in a mocking tone. "I don't even know why I said that."

"You're not going to kill me, are you?" he said.

"For now."

Adam allowed a hint of a smile to trace its way across his face.

"That's good," he said. "Comic relief. We could use some of that."

She smiled back, but it was all wrong. A beautiful rock with creepy-crawlies underneath when you lifted it up.

"So we're in a hell of a bad way here, huh?" she said.

She hitched her rifle onto her shoulder and leaned against a pickup truck in the parking lot of the clinic.

"Yeah," Adam said.

"Lately, I'll forget what's happened," she said. "I'll be doing something, eating dinner, whatever, and it'll seem like it's something I've been doing forever. Then I'll see something. A body. A pileup. And it all comes back. You know what I'm saying?"

Adam nodded.

"Anyway, I'm headed to St. Louis," she said.

"What's in St. Louis?"

She removed a pack of cigarettes from her breast

pocket and lit one. She took a long drag; twin plumes of smoke streamed from her nostrils. "Smoke?"

"No thanks."

She tucked the pack away.

"I was in New York when it went down," she said. "The Bronx. Couple of days before everything collapsed, we got an order from on high. Said the CDC had set up a testing facility in St. Louis and that anyone still healthy should head there for testing."

"Why St. Louis?"

"Beats the hell out of me. Anyway, I didn't realize how bad it was until I got out of New York. I was kind of hoping it was burning itself out the farther from ground zero it got."

"It's everywhere."

She flicked a peg of ash onto the ground.

"Yeah, that's what I'm figuring out. God damn."

He expected her to tear up then, but she didn't. She smoked the cigarette in silence, down to the nub, and then she crushed it under her boot.

"Is the St. Louis thing for real?"

"No idea. But I've got to find out for myself. This might be the last thing I do as Captain Sarah Wells, U.S. Army, so I plan to see it through to the end. Probably a wild-goose chase. But I've got to do it."

St. Louis.

"Anyway, what about you?"

"Got my own wild-goose chase."

"Care to share?"

He was struck by how forward she was and found himself a bit reluctant to talk about Rachel. He was afraid that if he verbalized it, it would sound far crazier than when it was just him thinking about it. Part of what kept him going was that it didn't seem crazy to think she was still out there, still alive.

"Got a message from my daughter in California," he said. "About a week ago."

Sarah scrunched up her face and tilted her face to the sky as she worked out the timing in her head.

"And she was still alive?"

"Said she was headed to her stepdad's condo in Lake Tahoe."

The conversation petered out, and they stood there in the August sunshine, an awkward silence pushing a wedge between them. Adam didn't know what to say. He really just wanted to get back on the road.

"Can I make a suggestion?" she asked.

"Sure."

"Let's team up," she said. "Head west together until we get to St. Louis."

Adam scratched his face as he considered her proposal.

"Look," she said, "someone needed to say it. It's goddamn dangerous out here. People are gonna have to start working together."

Adam tried to analyze the dilemma rationally. But

as he did so, he felt his eyes droop, and it made him realize how hard it had been by himself. He couldn't remember the last time he'd gotten a decent night's sleep, which had made getting by in this world that much tougher. But was this the right person to team up with? Would it jeopardize his own quest? There was no way to know when or if their interests would diverge, and how they would handle such a development. And then he thought about the fox and how it had snuck up on him with no warning and how next time it might be someone slicing his throat while he slept because there was no one to stop that from happening anymore.

"OK."

## 5

A t first, Erin Thompson had been relieved when they'd found her wandering across I-235, about sixty miles west of her home in Des Moines. Her fair skin had burned in the merciless Iowa sun, healed and then burned again, leaving behind a ragged quilt of newborn pink skin against sun-scorched ivory. She was starving and dehydrated, but she'd barely noticed, having devolved into a borderline catatonic state in the wake of the plague.

Erin and her husband, a pastor named William Thompson, had been living with their twin four-year-old boys in the small two-bedroom ranch subsidized by the First Presbyterian Church in Des Moines when the plague had hit. Jason, her youngest by eight minutes, had succumbed first, on August 13; his brother Billy had followed on August 14. By then, the pastor himself was gravely ill, and Erin had been absolutely out of her mind with grief. Willie had tried to soothe her, even when he'd been in Medusa's death grip, assuring her that it was all part of God's plan, that He was bringing them all home.

And when they were all dead, all laid up in their beds because she didn't know what to do with them, and they'd long since stopped responding to emergency calls, she sat there with Willie's body, cursing him for leaving her here, unsaved, while the three people she'd loved best, whom she'd given her life for, were rollicking with Jesus. And when she didn't get sick, she hated God, she hated Willie, she hated everyone and everything and she believed she had been forsaken. Apparently it hadn't been enough to be a doting mother and loving wife, giving up her career as a schoolteacher to do her duty as a Christian homemaker, even going through marriage counseling with Willie after she'd found those e-mails he'd exchanged with their nineteen-year-old neighbor, who, along with her three brothers, mother and abusive stepfather, were now dead, like everyone else she'd ever known.

She stayed in the house for another week, barely eating or sleeping, consuming just enough to stay alive. She drank from the tap, neither knowing nor caring whether the water was safe to drink. One day, she wandered the three blocks to their church, where she found it full of the dead. People who had come seeking salvation, relief, cure, something and received nothing but a nice hot cup of *Fuck Off*. The hours slipped by in a foggy haze as sounds and screams from only God knew where peppered the night and the day. The power didn't go out in her neighborhood until August 22, and so as long as she kept the doors closed, the smell didn't get too bad. Not that you could really escape it anyway. She'd cracked the windows one morning to circulate some fresh air, but then the smell hit her, the thick, rich, dead smell barreling through like an invisible and angry presence. Then the power had gone out and the smell was everywhere.

With barely a thought in her head, she packed Willie's backpack with clean underwear, her Bible, and some beef jerky and hit the road on the morning of August 24. Like many other survivors, she left her home because she simply couldn't stay there any longer. She didn't know where she was going, or what she would do with the rest of her days. She was only thirty years old, and the prospect of another five decades in this dead world loomed larger with each passing day.

Her plan had been to take Willie's ancient Camry, but she abandoned that idea after she put the car in drive rather than reverse and placed the front end squarely into their garage door. Embarrassment and shame flooded through her as she climbed out, fully expecting to see her neighbors poking their heads out of their front doors to see what the hell all the racket was. But there was no sound other than the ticking of the engine and the hiss of the cracked radiator. She stared at the crumpled garage door, behind which was the accumulated detritus of eight years of marriage, the garage Willie had been talking about cleaning the same weekend he'd gotten sick.

So she'd left the car there, buried in the garage of a house she would never see again, and walked east. A week on the road, with no destination in mind, no plan, no nothing at all, had driven her close to madness. Outside Windsor City, she'd been approached by two middle-aged women who'd asked her to join them. "Strength in numbers," they'd said, but she hadn't even acknowledged them, she'd barely even looked at them, and now that she thought about it, they'd made hay pretty quickly away from her.

But she hadn't gone with them, and so she was by herself when the black Suburban had pulled up along-side her along I-235 right about the time the sun was at its highest, roasting and broiling. Until the door had swung open and she'd felt the chilly air spill out of the passenger compartment, she didn't really care whether she lived or died. But it felt so good, even with the furnace of the Iowa sun beating down her neck, and she wanted more of it.

The tinted window slid down, revealing the face of ... an angel? Maybe she *was* dying, Erin had thought, somewhat hopefully, and this was how God was sending for her. A black SUV. A fresh face there in the window, young, her thick brown curls tied back in a ponytail, studying her, perhaps even pitying her.

"Oh, sweetie," the woman had said, clapping a hand to her mouth as though she couldn't quite believe what she was seeing. This poor wretch.

The woman disappeared from view for a moment, and behind her, Erin saw a man at the wheel, facing forward, smoking a cigarette. When the woman re-appeared she had a bottle of water in her hand, the condensation glistening in the afternoon sun. Erin stared at it the way a pyromaniac might stare at fire.

"You thirsty?"

She held the bottle out for Erin, who approached the car like a frightened puppy being offered a treat. Erin took the bottle and drank it down in one fell swoop, unaware of how severely dehydrated she was.

"I'm sorry, but do you have some more?" she croaked out, the words slurred and muffled behind cracked, sunburned lips.

"Sure," the woman said. "Why don't you come with us? You look like you need a break."

Erin found herself nodding without the slightest reservation. They had cold water. What other treasures might they have?

The doors unlocked with a decisive *ker-chunk*, and

she climbed in. A delicious chill rippled across her body as she settled into the cool leather backseat.

"What's your name, honey?"

"Erin."

She yawned.

"You just rest," the woman had said.

She fell asleep almost immediately, the promise of cold water, endless bottles of cold water lulling her to the deepest sleep she'd had in days. How easy it had been to lure her in, no different than a gullible child lured by promises of delicious candy and lost puppies.

And maybe, she thought to herself two days later, strapped to this examining table, it would have occurred to her that she could've found plenty of water on her own, that she hadn't had to let it devolve to such a state. If any of these things had occurred to her during her self-imposed death march, she might still be out there, pulling herself together.

Or maybe they'd been her only hope.

She just didn't know. No one spoke to her or explained to her what she was doing here. At first, she had thought that these had been government health officials rounding up healthy people for testing. But when they'd etched the inside of her wrist with that strange tattoo, she quickly realized that this was something else entirely. No one wore protective suits, and there was none of that urgency she saw in those last terrible days, on the street, in the hospitals, on the news.

They were in a brightly lit antiseptic room, which resembled one of the examination rooms in the urgent care clinic she'd once frequented with the boys, as they'd negotiated the rough-and-tumble world of ear infections and croup and impetigo. The long counter was stocked with bottles of hand sanitizer, cotton balls and the various and sundry items one might expect to find in a doctor's office. But the walls were bare, bearing none of the full-colored glossies with an artistic rendering of the human heart or the inner ear canal. She wore a paper-thin hospital gown and nothing else. It was itchy and barely reached all the way around her waist. Her feet were in stirrups, restrained, leaving her exposed and about as modest as a porn star waiting for the cameras to roll.

Footsteps clicking along the tile floor drew her attention. She looked over to see the woman from the SUV approaching her, but with far less mirth on her face. A small medical kit was tucked under her arm, which she set down on the metal tray mounted to her hospital bed.

Erin smiled at her, but she did not get one in reply.

"So what's this all about?" she asked in as brave a voice as she could muster.

Still the woman didn't speak. She tied a tourniquet around Erin's arm and promptly drew three vials of blood. The vials were labeled and went into a plastic tube rack. Then the woman snapped on a pair of latex gloves, retrieved a speculum from the bag and set up shop between Erin's legs. Instinctively, Erin tried snapping her legs shut, but to no avail; the restraints held them fast.

"Hey, what the hell is going on here?" Erin barked. "Don't you touch me!"

Her pleas fell on deaf ears, and she felt a strong pinch as the speculum opened her up. She looked at the ceiling and bit down hard on her lip, hard enough that she tasted blood. She tried telling herself this was no different than her routine visit to her OB/GYN, with the super-friendly Dr. Brady, a young doctor who'd been about the same age as Erin. Her daughter had been about the same age as Erin's twins.

*(ALL DEAD NOW ALL DEAD NOW)*

But she couldn't. This felt bad, very bad, and she felt shame for letting herself be hoodwinked by the promise of fresh water and food and a nice place to lay her head. She squirmed and twisted; hot tears ran down her cheeks. The long cotton swab entered her, scraping at her insides, and she felt her breath coming in ragged gasps.

She closed her eyes and thought about her sons, her sweet, sweet boys who had loved Thomas the Tank Engine and Lightning McQueen and now lay dead in their bedrooms. Jesus God, why hadn't she buried them? Did she think they were going to bury themselves? And it all came to her, all at once, that her little boys were dead and gone and she would never again see them in this lifetime. The sobs exploded from her, so ferociously that the woman examining her scampered backward half a dozen steps. As she lay there, weeping, all she could hope was that one day they would be reunited in heaven.

Then a terrible thought broke loose in her mind, a runaway meteor breaking free of its asteroid field, and turned her veins to ice; the horror of it was so deep, so profound, that she began to shiver.

*What if she were dead and this was hell?*

The sobs evolved into howls now, as though the woman were murdering her.

"We're all done here," she said.

She packed away the swab sample and the vials of blood and fled the room like it was possessed by all the demons of hell.

Erin continued wailing as the idea took deeper root in her mind and continued to flower. The more she thought about it, the less far-fetched it seemed. What was more likely, that she had somehow miraculously survived a global plague, the mother-loving apocalypse, that she had really hailed from the very deepest end of the gene pool? Or that she was now facing the thing that she had feared above all else?

Damnation.

A lesson from a college class came roaring back to her. Her freshman year at Iowa State, she had taken philosophy, during which they had studied the principle of Occam's Razor, which posited that all things being equal, the simplest explanation was usually the correct one. No, she thought, that couldn't be. Hell was a place of fire and brimstone and eternal pain.

*Fire and brimstone. Fire and brimstone?*

What had been more fiery than the Medusa virus, burning its way through humanity like a candle left near a musty old curtain? And what judgment could have been worse than watching your sons, the very lights of your life, die before your eyes within hours of each other, with no way to help them, with no one there to help them? Rattled with fear, bleeding from every orifice, screaming for their mommy, who could do nothing for them but watch them die. And now left here with no one and nothing but her thoughts, free to replay the last two weeks until she died or went insane.

Her mind went blank, as though a circuit breaker had flipped. Her gown was rucked up to her hips, leaving her naked from the waist down, but she didn't care. She didn't care when he eyed her leeringly, she wouldn't have cared if he'd climbed up on top of her and had his way with her.

He yanked her gown back down and took her back to the dorms.

## 6

After joining forces, Adam and Sarah commandeered an old Acura, but Durham's westbound points of egress, including Interstate 40, Route 147 and Route 70, had been blocked either by traffic or military vehicles. They had burned the rest of that day trying to find another way out, to no avail. By the time they realized that they'd need to walk or bike out of town, the day was shot, so they spent the evening gathering supplies. That night, they slept in adjoining rooms of a Holiday Inn, and the next morning brought with it two choices: hoof it or bikes. Sarah had offered up her chopper, with Adam riding pillion, but he'd declined.

"Two types of motorcycle riders," he'd said. "Those who've crashed and those who will crash."

Sarah didn't push the issue.

They'd broken into a large sporting goods store in Durham, where they geared up for a long bike ride. Adam had needed to start from scratch, having left much of his gear behind during his desperate search for the rabies vaccine. So when they left the store two hours later, both were outfitted with backpacks, tents, sleeping bags, water bottles, energy bars, ponchos, waterproof matches, compasses, hunting knives, a GPS transmitter/receiver, and flashlights. They also stopped in a drug store and stocked up on toiletries. It was surreal for Adam. Simply taking the stuff had felt so foreign; he kept waiting for the police to swoop in and arrest them for shoplifting. But, of course, none did, and they pedaled out of Durham around noon on August 31.

Adam was hopeful that they'd be able to trade up to something with an internal combustion engine a little ways up the road, but they never found more than a few miles of highway that wasn't blocked those first couple of days in September. So they stayed on their bikes. The slow pace was maddening, but there was nothing Adam could do about it. Moreover, it limited the stock of supplies that they could carry at any given time, necessitating more frequent stops.

As they rode, Adam tracked the landscape passing by; he realized he was looking for some sign that the world had changed, that things looked fundamentally different. But the truth was that it all looked about the same. A grain silo rose up before him, growing larger as they drew closer, and then receding behind them until it was gone from view. A Target distribution center. A salvage yard. These things looked exactly the same. They saw no one, the countryside hauntingly empty.

The early afternoon of September 3 brought them to Kernersville, North Carolina, about seventy miles west of Durham. They ate lunch on the playground of the Kernersville Elementary School. There had been little chit-chat between them since their union, only what was necessary to keep the expedition moving westward. This, Adam supposed, was shock. Didn't matter who you were, what you'd done before, you didn't watch the world die without a little piece of you going with it.

After lunch, Sarah studied their map while Adam administered the second dose of his rabies vaccine. So far, so good in that department. The bites themselves had nearly healed and he'd seen no evidence of any strange new symptoms. The fear was still there, as though hermetically sealed, ensuring it would never decay or yellow or soften at the edges. He wasn't sure he wanted it to fade away. It was important he remember what happened. That he remember how far off the reservation they were.

He got up and walked around, the late summer heat pressing down on him. The trees full and green, a few leaves on the branch tips just starting to turn. The incessant buzz of cicadas. He touched each piece of playground equipment, feeling the heat absorbed deep in the wood, and it made him sad to think how there were no children here. Behind him, Sarah lit a cigarette, and while she smoked, he checked his iPhone for messages. The dreaded NO SERVICE icon flashed in the top left corner of the screen. It had been days since he'd pulled a signal; he figured the cell towers had finally gone down.

Sarah was crushing the cigarette under her boot when he made his way back to her.

"There aren't a lot of population centers west of here," she said. "It might be worth trying to snag a car this afternoon."

This perked Adam's spirits. He couldn't believe how little progress he'd made since leaving Richmond, and this was welcome news indeed. He needed a win, badly. The vehicles left in the parking lot were their first target, but they were all locked or missing their keys. They rode into the center of town and stumbled across a Jeep dealership. A few minutes of trial and error finally resulted in a hit – the keys to a new Jeep Grand Cherokee, just a few miles on the odometer and fully gassed. As they loaded their gear into the cargo area, Sarah tapped him on the shoulder. When he looked up, she tipped her head toward the main road. He looked up to see a car quietly approaching from the north. Behind him, he could hear Sarah readying her M4. His heart pounded.

A rotund middle-aged man jumped out of the car and sprinted toward them, his arms flailing about his head. He was wearing a nice pair of dress pants, but he was shirtless and in bare feet; his shoulders and face were badly sunburned. Adam did not think the man was much in his right mind.

"They're here!" he yelled as he drew toward them. "They're here!"

"Whoa, whoa!" Sarah said, stepping out from behind Adam, making sure her machine gun was visible to all. "Take it easy, big guy!"

"They're here!" he said again. "They're here now!"

The man was becoming hysterical, his face cycling through about eight different shades of red. A bubble of mucus inflated from his left nostril as he repeated his warning again and again.

"They're here!" he yelled again, dancing in place, almost as if he had to go to the bathroom.

Adam glanced at Sarah, who just shrugged her shoulders.

"They're here," he said again, sinking to the ground. "They're here to kill us all."

Then he was curled up into the fetal position, bawling, howling, as though Adam and Sarah were ritualistically disemboweling him rather than simply watching him. Adam knelt down next to him.

"You OK, buddy? Who's here?"

He continued to howl.

"Let's calm down a little," Adam said. "You're safe."

Howls. Screeches.

Adam tried consoling the man for another fifteen minutes, but he simply could not reach him. He patted him on the shoulder. Nothing. He asked him for his name. Nothing. Every minute or so, he'd call out his warning and then retreat back into his catatonic state.

"Adam," Sarah said.

"What?"

"We need to get moving."

Adam dropped his chin.

"I know."

"Hey buddy," Adam said to the man. "We're gonna hit the road. You're welcome to join us."

"Here," the man said. "Here now."

"I can't leave him here," Adam said. "He needs help. Help me lift him in the car. He just needs some rest."

"You sure?" Sarah asked.

"We'll keep an eye on him. Grab his legs."

Adam slid his arms underneath the man's underarms while Sarah hooked hers around his legs. As they lifted him off the ground, the man bucked like a bronco. A runaway fist clocked Adam's ribcage, and the man was up and running and flailing about again.

"They're here!"

He ran back to his car and climbed onto the hood, where he continued his sermon, this time in earnest.

"THEY'RE HERE!"

Adam's head hurt.

"Let's go," he said to Sarah.

Sarah took the first shift and guided them back toward the interstate, the shouter's pleas booming in the giant stillness.

"They're here!"

They were two miles up the road before the man's voice faded away. Adam wondered what would become of him and those like him. How many people were out there right now, falling apart, unable to cope with the enormity of what had happened these last few weeks?

In the ordinary quiet of the car, things seemed almost normal. The air conditioning worked. An album by a band called the *Tattered Remnants* spun in the compact disc player. Just another road trip along a forgotten stretch of highway. Again, chit-chat was kept to a minimum, the experience at the dealership unnerving them both.

Fortunately, as Sarah had predicted, the roads northwest of Kernersville were clear. They drove deep into the wilds of North Carolina, toward the mountains. Adam's unease grew as evening approached, the sun tracing its eternal route through the sky, inching its way toward the horizon. He was still having a hard time at night, when the panic would rush through him as darkness spread across the landscape. It was almost palpable; watching the sun dip toward the horizon was like having his head pushed underwater, unable to breach the surface. He'd find himself clinging to the last bit of light as it leaked from the sky, almost willing it to freeze in place. This new world was crappy enough in the late-summer sunshine. Nighttime in a world of the lost was almost more than he could bear.

"Storm's coming," Sarah said.

Adam glanced up at a ridge of purplish clouds stretching toward the horizon. A storm. He'd loved thunderstorms once upon a time, but now it was just another thing to worry about.

"We may want to think about finding real shelter tonight," she said.

Adam's pulse quickened as Sarah pulled onto the shoulder. Finding shelter was something new. Something different. And anything different in this new world could be bad. Deadly, even. Adam looked down at his lap as Sarah studied the map from the glove compartment.

"This next town looks like our best bet for tonight. We can stock up on supplies."

"Oh, shit, we forgot to get them in Kernersville," Adam said.

"I know," Sarah said. "That scene with that guy just freaked me out."

They curled off the interstate and passed an empty park to their left, the susurration of the tall grasses audible in the giant emptiness. Just beyond, a large sign welcomed them to Walkertown.

"There's a little market up ahead," Sarah said.

Sarah pulled into the parking lot of Hall's Grocery and shut off the engine, which ticked and hissed as it cooled, the sound huge, almost embarrassingly so.

"You wait here," she said. "I'll get us something to eat."

"You shouldn't go alone," he said. "It may not be safe."

She patted her M4 rifle. "I won't be alone. Besides, you can keep a lookout."

She got out of the car, stretched, and went inside.

While she gathered their dinner, Adam fiddled with the vehicle's satellite radio hookup, edging his way across the spectrum, earning nothing but mild static for his efforts. He'd subscribed to the service himself, passing the time behind the wheel with the Bob Dylan channel, the '90s channel, Howard Stern.

*Was Howard Stern dead?*

That was a weird thought to have.

He took big, shallow gulps of air, sweet evening air, and he had to laugh at himself. He was still giggling a little when Sarah emerged from the store, a sack of groceries tucked under her arm.

"Something funny?" she asked.

"Just laughing at our little predicament here," he said. "Because this is some crazy shit we are dealing with."

This earned him a thin smile, but nothing more. As she stood there, smiling her thin smile, shockingly unfazed by the disaster, a bolt of anger swept through him.

"How are you so calm?" he snapped.

"What are you talking about?"

"We're standing in a worldwide graveyard, and you don't seem the least bit put out. How is that?"

The smile disappeared.

"I don't know what you're talking about," she said.

"Everyone you and I have ever known is dead! You get that? Dead!"

A sneer of disgust curled up on her face.

"Oh, I get it all right," she snapped back. "More than you'll ever know."

"What's that supposed to mean?"

"None of your goddamned business. Do you want to eat or not?"

The fight went right out of him, a balloon floating away from a child's hand.

"What the hell."

She sat down on the curb as the day's last light ebbed out of the sky. Adam switched on the headlights, bathing the storefront with a harsh white glow. Inelegant, perhaps, but better than the dark. Way better than that. He sat down next to her, quiet, as she picked through the paper bag, emblazoned with the Hall's Grocery logo. She handed him a can of spaghetti, a kid-sized cup of applesauce, a pack of Oreos and a lukewarm bottle of beer. He studied the label, AMB Pale Ale, a brand he didn't recognize.

"Sorry the beer's not cold," she said.

"Drank my share of warm beer," he said.

He twisted the cap off, priming his ears for the hiss of carbonation as the seal was broken. They clinked bottles, and he took a long pull. It was shit beer, truly wretched stuff only a college freshman could love, but it was still beer.

Sarah belched, loudly, and set the bottle down next to her.

"You'll forgive the lady."

"Sure."

He rolled the can of spaghetti between his hands, taking comfort in the weight. Sarah popped open her can and dug in with a plastic spoon. The tangy aroma of the tomato sauce tickled his nose, but not in a particularly good way, and he decided to pass on the pasta course.

"You need to eat," she said. "Keep your strength up."

"Think I'll pass tonight," he said, patting his midsection. "Watching my weight."

The joke fell flat, and she continued to eat her spaghetti.

Eventually, he ate the applesauce and the Oreos and then washed it down with the rest of his beer. When he was done, he got up and began stuffing the remains of his dinner into the trashcan posted at the front door. Then he stopped, his hand holding the heavy plastic flap open.

"God dammit, I'm such an idiot," he muttered.

"What?"

He wasn't even listening now, as he stewed in his juices, marinating in the annoyance of his cleaving to the old ways, dumping his trash as though the county sanitation department would be along in the morning to empty the cans out.

"This fucking shit!" He tipped the can over, sending it clattering onto the concrete walkway in front of the store. The lid came loose, and a coil of hot, stinking garbage oozed out, waiting for a garbage truck that would never come. Adam picked up the lid and flung it into the door, shattering it into a million pieces. The tinkling of fracturing glass echoed through the parking lot, and he stood there, watching the shards rain down onto the sidewalk in front of the store.

"Feel better?" she asked.

He stood there, his hands on his hips, his breath coming in ragged gasps. He felt his legs buckle, and he dropped to his knees, shivering, sweating. His heart thrummed, and his breath was catching in his midsection. His stomach hurt. Maybe he needed to go to the bathroom. Hell, maybe he was finally dying of Medusa.

He felt Sarah's hand on his back.

"Hey," she said softly. "Hey. It's going to be OK."

He rolled back onto his seat and pulled his knees to his chest. Hot jets of shame flooded through him, falling apart like this in front of this woman. Come on, Fisher. Come *on.*

He looked into her eyes. They were clear, calm, flat hunter-green pools. No hint of panic, no indication she was unable to handle this pitch the universe had uncorked at them. That's what it was about her. A preternatural calm. Where did it come from?

"I'm gonna run inside the store for a minute," Adam said. "Want anything?"

She shook her head.

Adam stepped inside the store. It was dark and humid. He shone the flashlight across the aisles, across the rack of postcards, the dead cooler full of soft drinks, the weekly newspaper stacked at the front so out of date that the headline read *Early Start to Flu Season*. He opened his wallet and withdrew all the cash inside, some sixty dollars. He left it on the counter and weighted it down with the collection jar. He didn't know why he did it. It was a horribly futile gesture, he knew that, but it made him feel better all the same.

Maybe he'd eventually get used to the fact that everything, everywhere was simply there for the taking. But it still seemed wrong.

"Want to talk about it?" she asked when he got back outside.

He looked back and saw her watching him, maybe studying him.

"I don't even know what to say," he said. "I mean, I want to say something, I feel like I should say something, but nothing comes out.

"I mean, what the hell is this?" he said, spreading his arms wide, feeling it all pour out of him, like his sanity had been inside a cup that had tipped over. The scale of it, the everything-ness of it, had pushed and pushed and pushed down on him, the pressure growing like air in a balloon.

She got up and brushed her hands on her pants.

"What's the first thing that comes to mind?" he asked.

She looked up at the sky and let out a long sigh.

"I guess I can't help but wonder what the hell happened."

"Fair enough," he said. "If it makes you feel better, I'm a doctor, and I don't have the first damn clue."

"A doctor? Not sure if that makes me feel better or worse."

He supposed he could understand; if a doctor

couldn't explain what happened, that was a pretty sorry state of affairs.

"Can I ask you a question?" Adam said.

"Sure."

"Did you ever feel sick? Did you ever experience any symptoms of Medusa?"

Her eyebrows popped up.

"Now that you mention it, no, I didn't," she said. "I kept imagining it, that I was coming down with it, but I never did."

"Me either," Adam replied. "Now it's possible that we did experience symptoms but that they were so minor that we didn't notice them."

"Is that important?"

"At this point, probably not," he said. "I'm not a virologist or infectious disease specialist, so this isn't really my area of expertise. But I'd love to know why we survived."

"I came through Philly, Baltimore, and D.C. before I made it to Raleigh," she said. "Barely saw a living soul. Heard folks. Voices carrying on the wind and whatnot. You were the first person I'd talked to in a week."

The image of the crowded northeast corridor emptied out made Adam's head spin. The virus would've spread fast, so fast, there.

"What kind of doctor are you?"

"OB/GYN."

"Babies."

"Yep."

She became silent, eyeing Adam, more looking through him than she was at him.

"Will babies get it?"

It was an important question, possibly the most important question of all, and he was disgusted with himself for not considering it. Pregnant women out there in the big empty. There was no way to know whether a fetus would survive its mother's exposure to the virus. And if the baby did survive to delivery, there was no way to know if she'd survive outside the womb. Adam just didn't know enough about how Medusa worked.

"Will they?" she asked again.

"I don't know," he said. "I really don't know."

"Aren't you the big party pooper?"

"I guess," he said. "I feel stupid that it hadn't crossed my mind."

"Maybe you didn't want it to cross your mind."

"Maybe."

"Well, Doctor, here's another question."

"Shoot."

"Why *are* we still here? Why were we spared?"

"Luck. Genetics. No virus is one hundred percent fatal. Well, maybe rabies is."

"What about God?"

This took him by surprise. It was the first time he'd even considered the theological implications of what had happened. He didn't like the fact that he was being sloppy and careless in his thinking.

"What do you mean?"

"What if this was God's judgment?"

He stood there, unsure of how to answer.

"You believe in God?"

When he didn't answer, she smiled.

"Look, I know that's probably getting a little personal, but I think we can do away with societal niceties for now, don't you?"

She was right.

"Some doctors can reconcile their faith with science," he said. "I never could. I've read the Bible. I minored in comparative religion in college. It never took. I'm sorry."

"Why're you sorry?"

He laughed softly.

"I don't even know. It feels like I should be sorry about something. What about you?"

"I used to believe in God," she said. "Once upon a time. I don't know anymore."

"Well, if there is a God, He spared you, right?"

"Maybe we weren't the ones who were spared."

He hadn't thought of it that way. The idea she'd been left behind by her God must have been a terrifying one indeed. It was a hard thing to process, even if it was a concept he didn't buy into himself. He didn't think the Bible was anything more than a fairy tale, written and massaged through the centuries by history's winners. And she had a point. Maybe they had drawn the short straw.

"Why don't we change the subject," she said once the silence had begun to metastasize into awkwardness.

"Good idea."

"How far is it to St. Louis?"

She studied her map for a moment, chewing her lower lip as she did so. He watched her, and he found himself staring into her green eyes again. As he did so, his breathing slowed, and his heart decelerated.

"About six hundred more miles."

"Jesus. It's taken us three days just to get this far."

"Well, we have to stop thinking like we used to," she said. "We can't assume we'll always be able to drive every mile from here to St. Louis."

"I guess you're right," Adam said.

"You sure you don't want me to teach you to ride a chopper?"

"I'm sure."

They were quiet a moment.

"You really think there's anything in St. Louis?"

Her face darkened.

"No, probably not," she said, her eyes cutting away from his. "But I gotta do it. Who knows? Maybe we'll get lucky. Maybe they have roast turkey and mashed potatoes."

"Chocolate milk?"

"Chocolate milk for you," she said. "Icy cold chocolate milk."

It was full dark now. Adam got up and stepped clear of the headlights' glow, into the inky darkness of the night. As he gazed across the undulating hills, the blackness stretched on forever. He tilted his head skyward and saw a blanket of stars twinkling in the night, a handful of diamonds tossed against black velvet.

He was glad to be alive. He was glad they'd teamed up (*those eyes, those green eyes!*). Standing here, watching the world continue to spin on, the way it always had, made it a little easier to believe that Rachel was still alive out there, maybe looking up at the same sky. He pretended it wasn't three hours earlier in California, where sunset was still hours away, and imagined she was looking at these same stars. Maybe she'd met up with other survivors, maybe she wasn't alone, questioning her sanity, wondering what the hell had been the point of surviving.

An hour later, they were camped out in the gymnasium of a local elementary school, listening to the hard rain thrum the roof, deep, throaty booms of thunder rolling through the ether. He tried not to think about Sarah, over there in her own sleeping bag, about her eyes, about her calm. But he thought about her until he fell asleep.

## 7

God, he was thirsty.

Yesterday, the thirst had started as a little gumminess of the lips, a little stickiness in the mouth, that realization that it was already afternoon and you hadn't had a glass of water all day. Easily fixed in the old days. You just plopped your glass under the tap, and voila, thirst quenched. But it wasn't the old days. Now Freddie's mouth was dry, an old cotton ball. His eyes itched like hell, and his piss smelled metallic.

They'd run out of water two days ago, and they hadn't been able to find any since. They were in the kitchen of a Taco Bell on the morning of September 6, just outside Murfreesboro, Tennessee, testing yet another kitchen faucet, befuddled by the lack of running water. This was the fourth different faucet they'd tried that day, and so far, all the taps had withheld their bounty.

Freddie held his breath as Caroline, leaning on her crutch, opened the spigot.

*Rat-tat-tat-tat-tat.*

The deathly rattle of dry pipes.

She shut the faucet and looked up at Freddie.

His stomach clenched with frustration.

"Dammit," he said. "Maybe it's because the power is out everywhere."

"No," Caroline said. "The electric pumps just move the water from the source to the treatment plants and then into the reservoir. But from there, it's mostly gravity pushing the water from the tower through the pipes. So the water should be running as long as there's water in the tower."

"Maybe the tower is empty," Freddie said.

Caroline rubbed a finger along a dry lip.

"Maybe," she said. "If we could just find some bottled water."

They'd been on their way to St. Louis when the water issue popped up, angling northwest through the Tennessee Valley, placing all their hopes into the government flier they'd found flipping through the deserted streets of Chattanooga. Caroline had latched onto the idea like a talisman. As her due date drew closer on the horizon, she was becoming increasingly desperate to see a doctor. Freddie hadn't been crazy about St. Louis, which, at best, would be a chaotic, confusing mess, and at worst, a hot, stinking graveyard like every other town they'd passed through.

But he went along with the plan because it gave them a goal to shoot for – even if this journey wasn't draining the emotional abscess that had formed in the wake of the plague. And besides, he thought they'd be safe because an NFL linebacker, even one who couldn't make a roster this year, was still a terrifying physical specimen for the average person. If nothing else, any troublemakers or ne'er-do-wells would probably not want to chance it, move onto someone they could rob or murder without too much effort. Not even post-apocalyptic highwaymen wanted to deal with hassle. But he would do it for her. Besides, he didn't relish the idea of delivering Caroline's baby by himself.

They were still traveling in the pickup truck that Freddie had intended to die in. Occasionally, they'd hit an unplayable lie, a stretch of highway that was just too clogged with dead traffic, and they have to backtrack and find another way. But there was no choice – her broken leg didn't leave them any other options. And the truth was, it was safer this way. As the days passed, Freddie had become increasingly conscious of the fact that while it had killed a lot of people, Medusa hadn't killed everyone. A few days earlier, they'd come across a dead backpacker along I-24, his throat slit from ear to ear. A harsh reminder that he and Caroline weren't alone in this shitty new world.

After striking out in the Taco Bell, they went back outside and set off again, bouncing from home to business to restaurant, looking for any water at all. In one law office, they found the office water cooler about one-eighth full, but a thin layer of algae had formed along the surface. They hit two grocery stores that day, but the shelves had been stripped clean of bottled water, soda, and juice.

Then they had turned their attention back toward the homes, ignoring the taps, the thirst deepening, digging down into their minds. Freddie's panic began roiling like a pot of water forgotten on a hot stove. Caroline was right, he thought. They'd find a stash of bottled water soon enough. But a search of two dozen homes had turned up nothing. Plenty of food stocked away, enough canned goods to keep them fed for months, if not years.

But the water.

It made sense, he supposed. Once the distribution networks collapsed, there would've been no more deliveries here; whatever bottled water was still on the shelves probably would've been snapped up in a hurry. In fact, people might have drunk the bottled water even when the taps were still running.

They found a twelve pack of Mountain Dew at one house, which they'd drunk greedily, but that was just robbing Peter to pay Paul. The soda provided a brief respite from the dry mouth, but the thirst returned within a couple of hours and in greater force. The sugar would dehydrate them even faster than before, putting the discovery of water at even more of a premium.

"How is this possible?" Freddie had blurted out as day began to soften into twilight, his anxiety rising. He was annoyed with himself. They should've abandoned Murfreesboro and pressed ahead; certainly they would've found water a little farther up the road. But now they were committed. He was exhausted, and his mind was cloudy from dehydration. Wouldn't that be something, he thought. To die of thirst in a land obsessed with bottled water.

At dusk on September 8, they came across a gated community in the western suburbs of town. Freddie inched his way into the neighborhood, guiding the pickup around a *de facto* roadblock of luxury sedans and sport utility vehicles. Perhaps the residents' last-ditch attempt to quarantine themselves from the world disintegrating around them.

He didn't relish the idea of conducting a house-to-house search in the dark, but he couldn't wait. Caroline was badly dehydrated, and the truck was nearly out of gas. He didn't know how long it would take to find the keys for another gassed-up vehicle, and he wasn't sure they had the time to spare.

A wide road bisected the subdivision, which was not unlike Wyndham, where Freddie had lived with his girls. God, he missed them terribly. If only there were an antibiotic to snuff out grief. His sleep came in fits and starts, and the same dream tormented him nightly, over and over, his daughter's last moments in that stinking, sweat-stained, blood-soaked hospital bed.

Large colonials lined the avenue, huge sprawling homes on at least half an acre each. The once well-manicured lawns had started to unravel, reverting to their natural state. For all the time and effort and money pumped into landscaping, the average American lawn was in a goddamn big hurry to let itself go.

He stopped at the first house on his right, dark and foreboding. The moon was full tonight, thank God for that, spreading out a luminous silver blanket across the land.

"Where are we?" Caroline said, startling him. He thought she'd been asleep.

"Gonna try and find some water," he replied. "Wait here."

"Can't this wait until morning?"

Her eyes were sunken and dry, which was all the answer he needed. He was unsure if she was the one who was afraid, or if she could smell the fear on him and was trying to spare him. He did want to wait until morning, he was goddamn sure about that.

"You need water," he said. "It can't wait any longer."

A full-body shiver rippled through her, despite the late-evening heat.

"Wait here," he said again. "If you need help, honk the horn."

"OK," she replied softly.

He smiled at her in the dark and stepped out of the car.

THE WINDOWS WERE DARK, the blinds shut tight. At the top of the porch steps, he paused and held his breath, listening for something, anything. Nothing. The door-knob held fast when he jiggled it, so he used the flash-light to break the decorative window flanking the side of the door. After clearing the stubborn shards of glass clinging to the window frame, he reached inside the gaping darkness and unlocked the door.

The house was warm, stifling, and a sour smell permeated the air. Before penetrating deeper into the house, he propped the door open to let in some fresh air. He swept the flashlight in a semi-circle around him, the white cylinder of light washing across the relics of a life once lived here.

His breath caught as the beam landed on a figure lying prone on a settee, an antique, high-backed thing in the formal living room. The figure, a woman, did not move as he drew closer. Just another plague victim. The body was bloated, her face swollen and clotted with dried blood. Freddie muttered a small prayer for this poor woman, who'd died on this couch, this really uncomfortable looking couch, and kept moving.

Two more bodies in the family room – an adult male in a recliner, a teenaged girl on the sofa. The man was still holding the remote control in his hand. Onto the kitchen, where Freddie found himself mesmerized by the family corkboard, mounted on the expensive stainless steel refrigerator. A reminder card for Steven's dentist appointment on September 14. Two tickets to the Titans-Steelers game the last Sunday in September. A picture of the family with a puppy; the photo had been date-stamped July 28, shortly before the virus had introduced itself to everyone. Freddie found himself priming his ears for the sounds or whimpers of a hungry puppy, but he heard nothing. Tears welled up in Freddie's eyes; somehow, these vestiges of the old world were harder to look at than the bodies dotting the wasted American landscape. This was what they had lost. The different threads of every different human fiber, from every race and ethnicity and creed that wove together to make the American quilt.

He opened the refrigerator, which expelled a warm puff of sour air, the breath of a ghost. Rotten vegetables and moldy cheese. Stale bread. A half-drunk bottle of

wine, missing its cork. But no water. There was a stair-
case at the edge of the house. As he made his way
downstairs, the flashlight slipped in his hands, and he
caught it, just barely. He paused to wipe his sweaty
palms on his pants. All of a sudden, he could feel his
heart pounding in his ribs, the blood rushing in his
ears. He was terrified of everything, all at once, of the
dark, of not finding any water, of Caroline dying on his
watch, of wandering the God-forsaken hellscape
America had become for months or years with each
second ticking by like an eternity.

He carefully negotiated the basement, spotlighting
each step he took. The cone of light bounced across a
water heater, a high-efficiency washer and dryer, a
foosball table, items that would never be used again.
The place was a wreck, looked like a bomb had gone
off. A sweep of the flashlight revealed blood spatter
everywhere. Filthy clothes reeking of human waste sat
in haphazard piles.

Then: victory. Atop a workbench, a case of bottled
water. He burst into tears upon seeing it, weeping as he
brushed his fingers against the still-intact shrink wrap.
The plastic crackled under his thumb. He hoisted the
case onto his shoulder and made his way back to the
stairs.

He was halfway up the steps when he heard the
truck's horn blow.

No, not just blow.

*Blast.*

He raced up the stairs and burst out into the dark front yard without a plan or a thought in his head other than a singular focus on protecting Caroline. A puddle of shattered glass pooled on the asphalt. The passenger door of their truck hung open limply like the broken wing of a bird; the car's interior light glowed with a sickly yellow hue, revealing its terrible secret.

Caroline was gone.

FREDDIE STOOD UNMOVING, not breathing, trying to process the scene in front of him. A sound to his right. A *scritch-scratch* sound, perhaps of something being dragged, and he recognized it as Caroline's pack on the ground, a sound he'd learned in their time on the road together. Her leg was still weeks from healing. Someone was carrying her into the night, her pack dragging behind her.

He set the case of water on the front seat and eased into the darkness, cursing it and thankful for it at the same time, nimbly carrying his massive bulk down the street, the way that had been praised and watched slack-jawed during all those Sundays on the gridiron. His eyes darted from point to point, target to target, looking for any clue as to Caroline's whereabouts.

Whoever had snatched her couldn't have gotten more than a thirty-second head start and now bore the burden of carrying an injured prisoner.

Stay calm, he told himself. Stay calm.

The roar of an engine shattered the silence, and ahead, maybe thirty yards, he saw a large vehicle, lit up like a Christmas tree, its headlights shining brightly in Freddie's face. Silhouetted against the stark white cylinders of light was a figure, stumbling along, the outline of a body slung over his shoulder. Freddie could just make out Caroline's pack dragging along the street.

If they got to the car, he'd lose her. He broke into a run, a full-throated sprint, chewing up the distance between him and his target like a lion closing in on an injured zebra. But it wasn't exactly like that, not really. The kidnapper held all the cards. And as if Caroline's captor had read his mind, he stopped and slowly swung around to face a rapidly closing Freddie.

"Take another step, and I'll kill her," the man called out. He said it matter-of-factly, without a hint of emotion or bravado, with a coolness that told Freddie that he would do exactly as he promised.

Freddie stopped on a dime, his knee aching. He was drenched in sweat, and his shirt clinging to him uncomfortably in the Tennessee night. Standing in the harsh blast of the car's high beams, how terribly exposed he was.

"She's hurt," Freddie said. "She'll just slow you down. And she's pregnant."

From the corner of his eye, just over the man's shoulder, he saw movement in the car. Time lost all meaning as he stared down his adversary, wondering if the sudden report of gunfire would be the last thing he'd hear in this world.

*Why hadn't they fired?*

The man shifted his weight from one foot to the other, and Freddie realized he was tiring from carrying Caroline over his shoulder. She hadn't made a sound, and Freddie wondered if she was still conscious. A few moments later, the man crouched down and lowered Caroline to the ground; instinctively, Freddie crouched with him. It seemed terribly important to mirror his opponent's maneuvers. She curled up in the fetal position, one arm protecting her abdomen, the second shielding her head.

A hiss from the car. It sounded like the second person was trying to communicate with his confederate.

"Huh?"

"MOVE!"

It hit Freddie like a bolt of lightning. The shooter hadn't fired because Caroline's captor was in his line of sight. As the man tried to process the order, Freddie made a break for them, hoping that he'd get there in time. A second later, a second too late, the man ducked out of the way, clearing the way for a barrage.

The shotgun roared, its tongue of flame bright and red in the darkness behind the sweep of the headlights. The round missed badly. As Freddie drew closer, the man pivoted just so in a vain attempt to escape Freddie's assault. Just ahead, Freddie heard the shooter fumbling with the shotgun, the clack of the barrel as he hurried to reload.

Body on body. The heavy, violent thwack of flesh on flesh, and Freddie was reminded of the big sacks, the big tackles, the terrifying and dizzying collisions of a sporting life gone by. He wrapped his big arms around his target and drove him into the blacktop with every ounce of his 265 pounds. Freddie felt the man's ribs break, a sensation that hit him in all the right places, lighting up his dopamine receptors.

It felt *good*.

The man whimpered underneath him, his body wrecked, but Freddie wasn't done. He felt alive, free, ready to act after weeks of reacting to the ladles of shit the world had been serving. He grabbed the man's ears, lifted his head off the asphalt and smashed it back down against the ground. The man's skull caved in like a watermelon, and he lay still.

But Freddie wasn't done.

No, not by a long shot.

Not at all.

These men had debts to pay now, debts owed to a society gone away, to see that even if the world lay dead in the gutter, justice would live on.

The shooter continued to struggle with the shotgun; Freddie could hear him whimpering as he seemed to grasp the collapse of their plan, wondering how things could have gotten away from them so quickly.

*"Nnnnnh,"* the guy was muttering.

Freddie wasn't even rushing anymore. He felt strong, easy, fluid. Six more steps brought him to the window, where he found his erstwhile assassin, still unable to load the shotgun. He was young, perhaps in his mid-twenties, his face still bearing the scars of recently healed acne. His hair was long, tied back in a sloppy ponytail. Tendrils of hair bounced loosely like broken springs.

He looked up at Freddie with wide, terrified eyes, Freddie's bulk and mass before him a monster from a child's bedtime story. Freddie simply stared back at him, unfeeling and uncaring. The man's fear had no more effect on him than a fly landing on his arm. He pulled him clear of the vehicle by the ponytail; the shotgun clattered to the ground, and his prisoner flailed his arms about as his body crashed to the ground in a heap. Freddie ripped the man's ponytail from his head, pulling it free in a messy clump. The man howled. Freddie retrieved the shotgun and loaded in its recalcitrant shells. When he was done, he placed the barrel of the gun under the bandit's chin.

"Please! I'm so sorry," the guy pleaded. His breaths came in shallow, ragged gasps.

"I'm sure you are," he said.

It wasn't anger or fear or even hate bubbling inside Freddie just then, as he eyed the skinny waste of space before him. It was disgust. The way one might look at a clump of dogshit on a well-manicured lawn. And what did you do with dogshit? You didn't leave it there to spoil the lawn, did you, to infect it with its parasites and bacteria? No, you got yourself a shovel and a bag and you cleaned it right up.

"Freddie."

The voice startled him. He looked back to see Caroline, who'd pushed herself up into a seated position. She'd propped herself on one arm, the other covering her abdomen.

"You OK?" he asked.

"I'll be fine. You?"

He didn't reply, because he knew damn well she wasn't asking about his physical well-being.

"Why don't we get going?" she said. It wasn't a question as much as an order.

The guy's eyes swung sharply toward Caroline, so hard they could have rocketed out the side of his head, as he sensed that perhaps he had a savior.

"And let him pull this stunt on someone else?"

"I think he's learned his lesson. Didn't you?"

He nodded vigorously, as if to underscore the fact he had most certainly learned his lesson, that he was a very, very good student who had paid very, very close attention to the teacher.

But Freddie wasn't even listening. He looked deep into the man's eyes, unsure of what he was looking for, not even aware if he would recognize it if it were there. Everything, Caroline, his grief, the stickiness of the late-summer night, fell away around him, as he zeroed in on the warmth of the shotgun's barrel in his left palm, the stiffness of the trigger under his index finger as he flexed it just so. It had felt good, killing the other guy, a scratch scratched, one that had been nagging him for so long.

"Freddie," she said again, this time with a little more heft in her voice.

"It's a shitty world out there."

The sound of his voice startled him.

"This will just make it shittier," she said.

He pulled the trigger.

## 8

T hey made good time after Walkertown, first cutting along Highway 66 and then continuing along Route 52 through the heart of northwest North Carolina. These roads, undoubtedly just as clear after the plague as they'd been before, made things seem almost normal. They passed through Mt. Airy, the sign at the town limits touting its heritage as the birthplace of Andy Griffith. Then they were in Virginia again, the extreme southwest tip that he had never visited. Adam couldn't help but laugh a little, that after all that time on the road, he was back in Virginia. A bit farther north, they looped onto I-77, and that was when they really started chewing up the miles.

Interstate 77 took them past Hillsville, Austinville, and Max Meadows, all lovely little towns, each as quiet and empty as the others. In Hillsville, they'd stopped and looked around, but they saw no one and heard nothing but the birds. A pack of dogs, looking mighty thin and hungry, had rolled up on them there on Main Street, sending them scurrying for the safety of the car. Then they were in the Jefferson National Forest, and it was here, for the first time since the plague had swept the globe, that Adam felt that his heart rate had dipped back below a hundred beats per minute.

He felt his ears pop a little as the Jeep climbed into the pass. Around them rose up every conceivable species of tree, pines and oaks and maples, thick green fingers reaching up into the sky. Adam rolled down his window, taking in the fresh air. He pulled onto one of the scenic overlooks carved out of the highway and got out of the car. To the north was a spectacular vista, a shimmering lake and a copse of enormous trees that appeared to have taken the passing of mankind in stride.

"Been a while since the world smelled this good," he said.

They spent the night there, opting to sleep in the car because Adam knew that black bears and bobcats roamed these woods. Adam slept deeply, as soundly as he'd slept since it all went down. The quiet was almost otherworldly, as though even the forest itself was paying mankind its last respects.

"How are we on gas?" she asked as they prepared to

set off that morning, a warm fog lining the edges of the road.

"Not bad," Adam said. "I think we've got enough to make it Lexington."

She laughed. "You're dreaming."

"Oh, really?" Adam said. "Care to make it interesting?"

"Fifty bucks says we don't make it to Lexington."

Another eight hours on the road left them running on fumes on the late afternoon of September 5. The Jeep ran dry on the outskirts of Lexington, Kentucky, hitching once, then twice, before quitting for good.

"You owe me fifty bucks," Sarah said as they began unloading their gear from the back of the Jeep. Most of the food and all the water was gone, a victim of the long trek through the wilderness of North Carolina and Virginia.

"No way," Adam said. "The bet was that we had enough gas to make it to Lexington. We are in Lexington."

"Oh, I beg to differ," she said. "We haven't reached the city limits. We may be near Lexington, but we are most certainly not in Lexington. And this Jeep is out of gas."

"Whoa, we never said anything about the city limits."

"You welching on a bet, Fisher?"

He dropped his jaw in mock horror. "I never welch

on a bet. But I'm a little short on cash. You think you can give me until next Friday?"

"Have it tomorrow," she said. "Or I'll have your legs broken."

Adam laughed at the absurdity of it all, at the way the world was now, the way that fifty dollars in cash would be better used as kindling for a campfire. He was still laughing as they made their way into town on foot.

It was becoming routine now; as they approached a new town or city, they tied bandannas around their mouths and noses to block the smell, even if just a little bit. The smell was what reminded them how deeply and how widely Medusa had cut them. It was what reminded them that in all those houses and apartment complexes and hospitals and nursing homes were the rotting bodies of countless millions, tens of millions, hundreds of millions of Americans. Someone's daughter or boyfriend or Nana. Now just a smell.

It was this thought occupying his mind as they trekked west along Interstate 64 into the city proper. There was a decent amount of stalled traffic in the eastbound lanes, headed out of the city, but the inbound lanes were mostly empty. That didn't surprise him, since there wasn't a whole hell of a lot behind them. They followed the exit off I-64 down to the main artery through town.

There was a new shopping development at the

edge of town, anchored by a series of big box stores. A Kroger, a Home Depot and a Target, all lined up like sentries. The parking lot was mostly deserted, but there were a few cars scattered about like a giant's forgotten toys.

"Hopefully this place hasn't been too badly picked over," Sarah said. "I'm hungry."

She checked her clip as they approached the entrance of the grocery store, always vigilant, as was her wont. Nothing escaped her, Adam had learned, and nothing rattled her. Either that or she had one hell of a poker face.

The doors had been shattered, leaving a puddle of glass bits on the sidewalk. A pungent smell wafted from inside, but it was different than the stench of human decay they'd become so used to. It was chokingly humid, pressing down on them like molten lead. He followed Sarah inside; it was a big store, and there was no way to know if anyone else was inside. They went aisle by aisle, starting in the produce section. The sight of hundreds of pounds of fruits and vegetables decaying in the bright and cheery produce bins was nearly as repulsive as any rotting corpse they'd seen on the road. Rancid juices from the burst skins had puddled on the floor and dried to a sticky residue. Adam had to stifle his gag reflex as they continued through the store.

They saw no one in the first eight aisles. On the

ninth aisle, Chips/Peanuts/Snacks, Sarah held up a fist and motioned around a rack of potato chips, stopping Adam in his tracks. He peeked around the end cap and saw a boy, maybe thirteen or fourteen years old, sitting cross-legged in the middle of the aisle, eating from a bag of Cheetos. He either hadn't heard them or didn't care that he had visitors. His hands and face were caked in orange dust. He was shirtless, wearing mesh shorts and flip-flops. His chest and arms were pockmarked with mosquito bites.

"Hi," Sarah said.

The boy glanced up at them. Then he went back to eating his Cheetos.

"You OK?" Adam asked, worried that they were about to repeat the scene from the Jeep dealership back in Kernersville.

The boy looked up at them again. Then he started crying. As Adam knelt next to him, the boy threw his arms around Adam's shoulders and hugged him tightly. He cried for fifteen minutes, never stopping, not once, never letting go while Adam soothed him. Finally, the crying began to subside, replaced by a series of long, deep breaths.

"What's your name?" Adam asked.

"Max," the boy said. "Max Gilmartin."

The boy's story was his own but not terribly dissimilar to theirs. Tales of surviving the plague were like snowflakes - no two exactly the same, but take just a step back, and they all looked identical: the news stories from the East Coast, and the virus crashing into Lexington like a runaway freight train, then the scenes from your average Saturday afternoon disaster flick playing out *ad nauseam*. He told his tale in one fell swoop, there in the chip aisle, his hand clamped around Adam's elbow as though afraid they might leave him there.

Max and his mom, who'd cleaned rooms at a local motel, had been living in a crumbling apartment complex on the south side of town when the outbreak began. Things had gone downhill in a hurry in Lexington's lower income areas, where people were packed together like rats, where it was hard enough to get medical treatment in summer, when cold and flu season had bottomed out for the year. His mom had died on August 20, and he had no other family nearby, leaving Max to fend for himself for the last two weeks. Since then, he'd been wandering about town, raiding grocery stores and residences for food, sleeping here and there, wondering what the hell he was supposed to do.

When Adam asked him if he wanted to join them, he started crying again.

"Can I bring my Cheetos?" he asked.

Adam smiled.

"Of course," Adam said.

He looked to Sarah for her approval.

She nodded.

"I like Cheetos, too," she said. "But you know what I really like?"

Max shook his head.

"Bubble gum," she said. "You grab the Cheetos, and I'll grab the gum."

IT TOOK them four days and a trying combination of walking and driving, but the trio finally hit the outskirts of St. Louis shortly after noon on September 9. They'd managed the last hundred miles in an Explorer, similar to the one Adam had left back in Holden Beach. The city's skyscrapers were foreboding monoliths, silent giants in the noonday glare. Quilts of middle-class neighborhoods stretched away to the north and south, looking perfectly ordinary on this September day.

They'd been on the road since first light, all of them anxious, perhaps even a little hopeful that the rally point was really there. There had been traffic, even a few pileups to negotiate, but each time, they'd been able to work their way around them. Karma, baby, Adam thought. But as they got closer to St. Louis, the absence of any human activity had him worried that they weren't going to find anything here either.

He and Sarah exchanged glances, their eyebrows

raised.

"What's wrong?" Max asked breathlessly from the backseat. "Is something wrong?"

Adam took a deep breath and let it out slowly. He had to remind himself that the kid was lost, adrift, looking for meaning in every word, every look. It was important to him that Adam and Sarah know the score.

"No," he said as gently as he could.

These empty lanes told him no one else was headed for the supposed rally point, that this center-piece of the Midwest, the gateway to the western states, was as dead as everything they'd seen to the east. The city's residents had tried to flee while they could, for all the good it had done them, and this was the residue left behind. Now Adam had all the information, all the pieces of the puzzle he needed to know that the disaster had been as complete as he had feared. Rachel's report from the West Coast, combined with his own observations on his westward trek gave him the nationwide perspective he'd been simultaneously hoping for and dreading. He realized he'd been hoping that the virus had mutated along the way to a less virulent form, something to help it keep moving and sparing certain parts of the country. But, to steal an analogy from the now defunct world of sports, the Medusa virus had elected to run up the score.

Not very sportsmanlike.

"Where's the rally point?" Adam asked.

"Supposed to be at Busch Stadium."

"Any idea where that is?"

"Not really."

"Think the GPS still works?" Max asked, pointing at the in-dash navigation screen.

"You know what? I bet it would."

Since the GPS wouldn't operate while the car was in motion, Adam drew to a stop in the breakdown lane and punched in the information into the touch screen. They sat silently as the computer processed the request, and when the female voice asked if she could program a route for them to Busch Stadium from their current location just as sweet and pleasant and unoffensive as could be, Sarah burst out laughing. Adam quickly followed, and before you knew it, the three of them were rolling.

"She seems chipper," Sarah said.

"No skin off her back, I guess," Adam said.

They laughed as they continued toward the city proper, through the slums in the east, once notorious in the magazines and Sunday newspaper features as one of the worst neighborhoods in the country but now on the same footing with all the rest. The buildings and cars looked small from this far away, like child's toys left behind on a playground.

A quarter hour later, the Mississippi River came up on them, wide and glassy that afternoon, lazily snaking its way through the heart of America. Adam, who'd never seen it in person, tried focusing on the road, but the river pulled on his gaze time and again. Boats, resembling toys from this distance, rocked in the still waters downriver.

"I just had the most random thought," Adam said.

"What?"

"Is there anyone on the International Space Station? What about a Navy ship or submarine out in the Atlantic? Or an oil rig down in the Gulf?"

"Jesus," Sarah said. "I hadn't thought about that."

"I don't understand," Max said.

"There could be people in all those places," Adam said. "People who weren't exposed to the virus. They could still be healthy. They might be out there right now, wondering what to do."

"What would happen to them if they came back?"

"I don't know," he said. "I really don't know. I don't know if we're carrying the virus inside our bodies. I don't know if it's lurking somewhere or if it burned off. Or if it's mutated."

His mind drifted to the world they'd be facing, and it was more than he could process. Traffic on the river itself would be nonexistent in the coming weeks and months, giving the river a chance to repair the environmental damage it had suffered in the last few centuries. Strange thoughts. Strange days.

"Look," Max said, pointing ahead.

They were approaching an overpass, atop which Adam could make out two figures staring out down across the highway.

"Holy shit!" Max exclaimed. "He's got a gun!"

Adam cocked his head for a better view and could just make out the glint of gunmetal in the sunshine. A round slammed into the concrete about twenty yards away, the report of the gun echoing off the automobile graveyard surrounding them.

"Jesus H. Christ!"

He yanked the wheel to the right.

"Stay calm," Sarah barked. "How's the road ahead look?"

Adam tore his gaze away from the overpass and peered down the highway. The dead traffic had thickened here like trans fats clogging an artery. He decelerated and slalomed his way around the abandoned vehicles. Another few seconds brought them directly under the overpass, just as the shooter prepared to fire.

"It's getting a little crowded here," he said, as a second shot shattered the windshield of an abandoned box truck in the eastbound lanes.

"He's firing blind," she said, a steely conviction in her voice. "He's not a good shot. Just take the next exit and drop down into the city."

Another shot exploded behind them, followed by a loud pop; the car shimmied underneath him and fishtailed.

"We blew a tire, we blew a tire!"

"Shows how much I know," Sarah muttered.

He eased off the gas and steadied the steering wheel until the car rolled to a stop in the middle of the freeway, not far from the exit ramp.

Then another shotgun blast.

"We're gonna have to run for it," Adam said, hoping he was covering the panic he was feeling.

"Max, swing your door open, but stay in the car."

"I don't wanna get out of the car."

He was ramrod still, his eyes shut tight, his hand clenched into little chubby fists.

"Max, it'll be OK. We're up against the jersey wall. We're gonna stay low, and the door will shield us. Max. We can't stay here. I'll make sure you're safe.

"Give me your hand," Adam said, reaching toward the kid.

Max shook his head violently, like a child refusing his medicine.

"Max," Adam said, his voice dropping in volume. "We're going to do this together."

Slowly, the boy slid his hand into Adam's; it was cold and clammy.

"Now with your other hand, swing the door open."

Max swung the door open. The edge caught the jersey wall, making a nails-on-chalkboard screech. Adam retrieved his gun from the console and nodded toward Sarah, who slipped out onto the shoulder with her M4 slung across her back. Max scurried over the center console and followed Sarah out the door. As Adam brought up the rear, a shell shattered the rear windshield. Max screamed.

"Stay low, stay low!" Sarah hissed. She squeezed off a burst at the overpass. The roar of the machine gun fractured the morning, its chatter making everything seem harder and more real. The shooter ducked below the railing, pushed back by the threat of Sarah's heavy gun. Sarah kept the gun trained on his position, and when he reappeared, she took his head off with a short burst from the M4.

They hugged the wall as they scampered east; Adam crab-walked, keeping an eye on the road behind him, listening for footfalls, the click of more shells being chambered. He didn't know if there was one potential killer or three or twenty.

He glanced up the road and saw the exit ramp fifty yards off. More gunfire peppered the afternoon air. Sarah waved Adam and Max past her. Then, using a shiny Lexus coupe for cover, she rose up and fired a burst from the M4 at the second shooter. Adam paused, Max's hand sweaty and tight in his own. Then he shimmied up next to Sarah and drew his gun.

"What the hell are you doing?"

"Helping," he said, although it came out more as a question.

"You ever seen combat?"

"No," he said.

"Get him the hell out of here," she said, nodding toward Max. "I'll meet you at the bottom of the next exit. Go!"

Adam pressed the butt of the gun to his forehead, his teeth clenched. Back toward the overpass, an angry voice bit into the air.

"Go!"

As he turned back toward Max, he spotted a figured closing in from the east, also sliding down along the jersey wall.

"Sarah!"

She swung her attention toward Adam as he gestured wildly to the east. Then she slipped around the front of the Lexus, staying low but leaving herself very exposed.

Adam fumbled with the gun, but it was slippery in his sweaty hands, which were moving in slow motion. The figure drew closer, but Adam still couldn't make the gun work. He might as well have been trying to defend himself and Max with a jar of peanut butter.

Then a stitch of gunfire slammed the man against the wall, and he slid to the asphalt, quite dead. Blood smeared the wall where his body had impacted it. Sarah emerged from between two cars in that lane, her gun still trained on the man.

She slid his gun away from his body with her foot, and Adam exhaled.

## 9

They made it unmolested to the bottom of the exit ramp and onto 4th Street, which ran north through the stadium area. Adam's heart continued to race in the wake of the little skirmish at the overpass, and he was having a hard time concentrating. He'd known such a thing was possible, even likely, as the world drifted away from the shoreline of civilization, but it had been so harsh and vivid and sudden that he'd barely been able to react. Why had it happened? To what end? The more he thought about it, the more he worried he wouldn't be long for a world like this. How Sarah had done it, he'd never know. She'd say it was her years of training that had kicked in, muscle memory, but it was more than that. It was something he didn't think he had.

"Look at all the bodies," Max whispered as they made their way north.

Max was right. There appeared to be an unusually high concentration of victims here.

"Adam," Sarah said. "Look over to your left."

Adam turned his head and saw Busch Stadium rising in the shimmering afternoon sun. Not twelve months earlier, this place had hosted the National League Championship Series, which the hometown Cardinals had lost in five games to the Washington Nationals. It was hard not to overlay his memories of baseball on top of the empty shell that lay before them.

They were on the stadium's east side now, cutting in between the stadium and the Gateway Arch Park to their right. Adam didn't know what they were supposed to be looking for, but it looked a lot like everything else they had seen. They passed a parking lot full of abandoned military vehicles. At the corner of 4th and Clarke, sandbags and a machine-gun battery.

"See anything?" he asked.

Sarah held her M4 tight.

"Let's find the main entrance," she said. "Stay close."

Dread crawled up Adam's back like a snake.

"There's no one here," Adam said. "We should get out of here."

"I've got my orders."

Adam held his tongue. There'd be no arguing with her. She had her orders.

They proceeded west on Clarke Street, moving slowly, their backs to one another to give them a 360-degree sweep of the area. As they fell into a rhythm, the silence engulfed them like a heavy blanket. They heard nothing and saw no one as they drew closer to the stadium's main entrance. The stench was horrific, deeper and stronger than Adam had smelled yet. Weeks of immeasurable human decomposition was finally peaking.

Sawhorses lined the front entrance of the stadium, but there was no one guarding them. Bodies of soldiers, some wearing gas masks, littered the concourse. The trio passed under the black metal arches, gleaming in the afternoon sun, up the ramp and into the bowels of the stadium. Shuttered concession stands and a dark souvenir store greeted them as they moved along the outer concourse. There were hundreds of bodies in here. Adam felt Max press his body up against him.

Then they were in the bleachers, staring out across the empty field, this dead cathedral to America. Thousands of bodies were scattered through the stands, their empty, bloated faces staring at them, waiting for a game that would never begin. The outfield grass had grown long and rippled in the afternoon breeze, but the infield was still groomed, the white lines marking the baselines still pristine. Tents bearing the logo of the Federal Emergency Management Administration lined the warning track, but they, too, were abandoned, silent. A few crows and vultures here and there, pecking at the remains.

"I just had to be sure," Sarah said, as they descended the steps.

"We should check the tents for supplies," Adam said.

A burst of birdcall above them, and Adam looked up to see the sky darken with hundreds of blackbirds swirling about like a cloud. They flew lazily, in circles, as though the offerings of carrion were so vast, so varied, they didn't know where to begin. A lifetime of dining on squirrels and field mice had been replaced with the greatest buffet line they'd ever seen.

As he watched the birds, his stomach swirled, the dead stadium a gut punch, more than he cared to admit. It had represented the last best chance that humanity still had a pulse, faint as it might have been, and seeing that it was gone left him dizzy. There was nothing. You expect something bad to happen, but there's still that tiny sliver of hope, stuck in your mind like a splinter, that it might still go the other way. But then the bad thing happens, and you're looking at it, and it's just as bad as you feared and there's nothing you can do. They stood there for a full ten minutes, long enough to feel the sun's rays grow uncomfortably warm on their necks and arms.

"Max, you ever been on a major league field before?" Adam asked.

"Uh, no."

"Follow me."

"What are you doing?" Sarah asked.

"Just taking a little break," Adam replied. "Ten, fifteen minutes."

"We should probably get a move on," Sarah said.

"I can't right now," Adam said. "I just need a break."

They found bats and balls and gloves in the Cardinals dugout. Adam threw fat batting practice pitches to Max, who had a nice, natural swing and even put a couple into the outfield. Around them, the empty faces of the dead watched them play baseball. Maybe this wasn't the wisest use of their time, Adam realized, but he didn't care. Rachel, if she was even still alive, was two thousand miles away, and what the hell, he might as well throw a little batting practice.

As he reared back to fire another pitch in toward the plate, Adam froze suddenly. Just over Sarah's shoulder, an enormous man was approaching them, carrying in his arms a wisp of a woman.

"Hey!" he barked. "This the testing center?"

Sarah turned to face the newcomers, her machine gun raised up and ready for business.

"Don't move!" Sarah called out.

"She needs help," the man said, dipping his chin toward his human cargo.

Then the man froze and took in the full scope of the scene before him. His head rotated from one side to the other.

Sarah looked over at Adam, who nodded toward her.

"It might be a trap."

"No!" the woman called out. "I'm pregnant!"

The news galvanized Adam like a shot of adrenaline to the heart. Pregnant. He got a good look at her swollen belly. At least thirty-five weeks along, Adam surmised. Close to full term, close to finding out up close and personal and that pretty goddamn soon whether babies were immune to the Medusa virus.

"It's OK," Max called out, holding his hands up high. "He's a doctor."

"Oh, my God, are you for real?" she said, bursting into tears.

The man looked down at the woman and whispered something to her; she nodded and squeezed his shoulder. He took her down into the dugout and propped her up on the bench. A makeshift splint framed her right leg.

Images of babies dying of Medusa flooded Adam's brain, and he didn't want to be anywhere near this woman. He didn't want them to know he was a doctor. He didn't want to be the one who couldn't do anything for her. What was he going to do, perform a C-section there in the dugout with some plastic cutlery?

They waited.

Finally, Adam followed them down the steps to the dugout and took a knee next to her. The floor was still sticky with tobacco dip and sunflower seed shells.

"You really a doctor?" she asked.

He chewed on his lower lip; he could just lie and say the kid had been making it up, and maybe Sarah would go along with him because she would understand he had some reason for doing so. But in the end, he couldn't.

"Yes."

He saw a big smile spread across the woman's face, and she gently placed her hands on her abdomen.

"Don't suppose you're an OB?"

"I am in fact an OB."

"Jesus. I guess this is my lucky day. Are you a good one?"

"Best in the city."

She laughed and broke into tears simultaneously.

He was glad they'd shared the joke. Humor was humanity's great glue, yoking people together for thousands of years. That was something, he thought, as he drew closer, keeping one eye on her massive companion.

"When are you due?" he asked.

A breeze rustled through the shadowy dugout, cooling them.

"September twenty-fifth."

"How's the pregnancy been?"

"Pretty uneventful," she said.

"Baby been active?"

She nodded.

"Rome burned, and he kept right on kicking," she said.

"It's a boy?"

"Yeah."

"Well, the kicking's good," Adam said. "Real good."

He pointed at her belly and held up his hands. "Do you mind if I examine your stomach?"

"Go ahead."

"You mind lifting up your shirt for me?" he asked, wanting her to be the one to expose her belly. "Just halfway so I can get a look at your stomach."

He gently palpated her stomach, feeling for the head. A moment later, he felt the baby squirm and roll, twisting away from his manipulations.

"Any allergies?"

"No."

"I'd feel more comfortable with an ultrasound machine, but things seem right on track. I'd say another couple weeks."

Her face lit up, and her eyes were wet with tears.

"Thank God," she said. "I haven't seen a doctor since July."

"Well, let's hope your luck holds out."

"Will you deliver the baby?"

There was no way around it. In this new paradigm, not doing his job would put her life in danger. Too many things could go wrong. People thought that delivering babies was a simple matter, and maybe in the grand scheme of things, across the giant sample size that had been humanity, it had been. Most babies and mothers survived their delivery. Most. But this woman would be playing against a stacked deck. It wasn't going to be easy for her with that broken leg, even with another two weeks of healing.

"Of course," he said. "I don't know how many obstetricians are running around these days. I can't promise you everything modern medicine could have delivered two months ago, but we'll do our best."

She reached out and squeezed his hand.

"Thank you," she said, tears in her eyes. "It's been a while since I've heard any good news."

Her eyes narrowed, and her face turned to stone. He knew what was coming, and he began working on an answer before the words were out of her mouth.

"Will the baby catch it?"

"You don't beat around the bush, do you?"

She gave him a wan smile.

"I'm not going to lie to you," he said. "I really don't know."

He searched for something to say, but anything else would have been superfluous, the wilted lettuce lying alongside the entree.

The thin smile disappeared.

"At least you're honest."

"We're probably past the point of lying to make each other feel better," Adam said. "Let's move on. How's the leg feeling?"

"I guess it's healing. Itches like hell."

"That's the bone stitching back together. Mind if I take a look?"

"Think we're getting to know each other pretty well, Doctor.... Oh my God, I don't even know your name."

"It's Dr. Fisher," he said. "But you can call me Adam."

"I think I'll stick with Dr. Fisher," she said. "At least until the baby comes."

"Fair enough."

"My name's Caroline," she said.

"Caroline, I'm sorry we're meeting under these crappy circumstances."

He examined the splint carefully, not wanting to jiggle the leg. There was a dull yellow bruise about the size of a silver dollar about midway between the kneecap and the ankle, and the flesh was slightly swollen.

"When did this happen?" he asked.

"About ten days ago."

"How?"

"Fell down some stairs," she said. "I guess I was lucky I didn't fall on my stomach."

"How's the pain?" he asked.

"It comes and goes," she said. "It seems to be getting better."

"Well, given the circumstances, I think you're doing pretty well. You let me know if he stops kicking."

He gazed up at her companion, who'd been watching him like a hawk, and extended a hand. He was enormous, an amazing physical specimen. A purple and gold LSU t-shirt was drawn tight against his massive chest. His biceps were cut like diamonds.

"Adam Fisher."

The man returned the shake, Adam's hand virtually getting lost in his paw.

"Fred Briggs."

Strangely, the name rang a bell for Adam, but he didn't know why. Certainly, he'd remember having met a guy this big, this imposing.

"So there's nothing here?" the man asked. He glanced over his shoulder and saw Sarah had joined them in the dugout; her M4 was still out, but much to Adam's relief, she had lowered the muzzle.

Freddie looked over at her, wiped a hand over his scalp, which was shiny with sweat.

"No," Adam replied. "Whatever was supposed to be here, it didn't happen."

A gunshot in the distance cracked the silence.

"We're headed for California," Adam said. "It's safer out on the roads than in the big cities. At the very least, it doesn't smell as bad."

"Why there?" Freddie asked.

"My daughter might still be alive out there," Adam said. "Had to give it a shot."

"You think the immunity is hereditary?" Caroline asked, her voice spiced with hope.

Adam weighed his response carefully.

"I really don't know," he said. "If she's still alive, it's possible there's a genetic component to it. I don't know if there are any other cases where a parent and child both survived."

"My kids weren't immune," Freddie said darkly. "They died just the same."

"Oh, Freddie," Caroline began, "I'm sorry. I'm so sorry. I didn't mean..."

He stomped up the dugout steps and toward the infield.

"What's his story?" Adam asked when they were alone.

"God, I've been such a pain in the ass," she said to Adam and Sarah. "I've been so worried about the baby and this damn leg that it never occurred to me to even ask about his family."

"Don't beat yourself up." Sarah said. "I'll talk to him."

Adam watched her follow Freddie, who had drifted over toward the concourse.

"Is this guy OK?" Adam asked.

"I know he's rough," Caroline said. "But he saved my life. Twice. I can't judge him."

Adam didn't know how to process that, so he let it slide for now.

"So what do you think about taking a little road trip?" he asked. "Free medical care the whole way. No co-pays."

"That is pretty tempting," she said, a smile spreading across her face. "I still can't believe you're a doctor."

He held up an index finger.

"Hang on."

He extracted his wallet from his back pocket.

"Still carrying your wallet?"

"Old habits die hard," he replied as he thumbed through the Visa card, the driver's license, the membership card from Sam's Club. A wave of nostalgia, a strong one, swept through him, as he thought back to the last time he'd swiped his debit card for a Starbucks coffee, the last time he'd run into a grocery store to grab a few things.

"Here."

He held out his Physician's ID card issued to him by the Virginia Commonwealth University Hospital. She waved him off, but he kept the card out, pinched between the index and middle fingers of his right hand. Finally, she took it from him and gave it a once-over.

"So there it is," she said.

"There it is."

Caroline burst into tears; she held a hand over her mouth and took several deep breaths, but she couldn't stop crying.

"It'll be OK," he said.

Even though he really didn't know that.

Gunfire peppered the afternoon again, this burst closer than the first.

"We need to get on the road," he said.

"OK," she said. "I'll come with you."

"You think your friend will join us?"

"Yeah," she said. "Yeah, I think he will. He's been so good to me. I don't know why. I've been shitty to him. Like I said, he saved me."

She paused, and her eyes welled with tears.

"It's been hard out there," she said softly.

"I'm glad you're coming with us," he said. "I think there's strength in numbers. Look, I don't know if my daughter is still alive. Maybe it's a pipe dream. But it gives me something to work towards."

Freddie resisted at first, but when he saw there would be no changing Caroline's mind, he dropped his objection to the two groups joining forces as a quintet. Adam still wasn't sure about him. He was wound tight, like old nitroglycerin. But despite his own personal loss, he'd been looking out for this woman he hadn't ever met before a month ago, putting aside any wishes or thoughts or wants or even needs for her benefit. That had to be worth something.

Freddie went to retrieve their vehicle while Sarah and Adam scoured the FEMA tents for supplies. It proved to be a bonanza. They found several cases of bottled water and dozens of MREs. Toilet paper. After loading the new supplies, they were off, winding their way back toward Interstate 64. By late afternoon, the city was behind them, the pickup truck chewing up highway as they headed west. In a couple of spots where the traffic was too snarled to negotiate, they had to double back and detour off the interstate, but there was a well-maintained access road paralleling the main highway.

Adam didn't know what to think, what to feel. He rolled down the window and propped his elbow on the door as Freddie slalomed around the dead traffic. Finding Caroline and Freddie, that had to mean something, right? What were the odds this pregnant woman, a few weeks from delivery, stumbles across likely one of the few surviving obstetricians in the country?

He was glad they found her, as much for him as for her.

He *was* a good doctor, as his boss Joe McCann had said that day, the morning he'd suspended him. The Baby Wall had been a testament to that. He could see their faces, their beautiful, innocent faces and he couldn't help but wonder if a single child from that wall was still alive. A flashback to the office, Joe mentioning offhand that he hadn't been feeling well that morning. Jesus, he thought, his skin crawling. Had Joe already been sick with Medusa? He'd probably seen a dozen patients in the office, countless more at the hospital, before he'd become too sick to continue.

This made Adam's insides clench with sadness, but at the same time, he was glad to be alive. He wasn't ready to die. How glad he was that there was a good chance that Rachel was still alive. That Caroline and her baby wouldn't have to do it alone.

He glanced back at Max, who had fallen asleep on Sarah's shoulder. For the first time since they'd met, his young face looked its actual age. It was smooth and unlined, as though all the stress and panic bunched up on his face had drained away like heavy rains into a storm drain. Caroline napped too.

The sun was warm on his elbow as the St. Louis metro area shrank rapidly in the mirrors, the urban terrain morphing into the western suburbs and far western exurbs. Ahead, the road was wide and open and clear, the air fragrant with the smell of rain. Dark clouds to the west portended afternoon thunderstorms.

They were in a hell of a pickle, he knew that. Each and every safety net all of them had depended on for decades was gone forever. Things could get bad in a hurry, as the thunderheads up the road well proved. The lightning flashed and the thunder rumbled gutturally in the distance, and he hoped it wasn't an omen of things to come.

## 10

<hr />

It was slow going west of St. Louis. Even when the roads had been clear, it was becoming increasingly uncomfortable for Caroline to travel, necessitating frequent breaks along the way. They used these breaks to scout for supplies, which required constant replenishment. Sarah took these opportunities to restock her chewing gum and Max's supply of Cheetos, which he ate nonstop. They probably couldn't let that go on forever, but for now, it seemed like it was OK. Caroline got in on the act as well, requesting ready-to-eat pepperoni. Adam loaded up on chocolate bars. Nothing for Freddie, though, which irritated Sarah to no end.

"Are you sure?" Sarah had asked, as she'd headed out on a supply run one afternoon. "Anything you want. My treat."

"Nothing for me," he'd said.

*Jerk.*

Approaching Kansas City on the morning of September 13, they'd encountered the worst traffic jam they'd seen since leaving St. Louis. Salina, about 180 miles to the west, had been their target that day, but the gridlock in Kansas City had forced them to abandon Freddie's truck, which, in turn, had created the problem of transporting a still-immobile Caroline. They'd spent much of the day looking for a wheelchair for her, and by the time they'd found one in a small hospital on the north side of town, the day was shot. On the plus side, Adam had assembled a bag of medical supplies he'd need on hand for Caroline's delivery.

So at dusk on the thirteenth, they'd set up shop near a heavy truck dealership just west of Kansas City. Beyond the dealership was a grassy plain stretching north to the horizon. Sarah and Adam checked the building, made sure it was clear. It was, and as an added bonus, it had running water and showers. The water was cold, ice cold, but that was fine with them. Sarah had stood under the water until she was shivering, until she'd scrubbed days of grime and grit from her body. She scrubbed until her skin was pink, until the smell of the soap seemed entwined with her DNA.

Freddie and Adam got to work making dinner while Sarah and Max conducted a sweep of the camp.

"How come we never stay in houses?" Max asked as they walked the perimeter.

"Well, Adam said it would be best if we stayed away from the cities and towns," she said. "Things aren't exactly very clean."

"Because of all the bodies, right?"

"Yeah. Because of the bodies."

"Can I tell you something?" Max asked.

"Sure, sweetie," she said as her eyes swept the desolate plains before them.

"I used to think the apocalypse would be cool," he said.

She smiled.

"It's not what you thought, huh?"

"I always thought it would be zombies," he said. Then, his voice softening: "Thought I'd be really good at killing zombies. I used to play this game called *Dead Men Walking* all the time. I feel so stupid. No, it hasn't been what I thought. It's been horrible."

"Know what?" Sarah said, softly.

"What?"

"You weren't the only person who thought like that," she said. "I knew some grownups who thought it would be cool for the world to end. Even some soldiers."

"Are any of them still alive?"

She smiled at him.

"No."

"Why do people think like that? Did they think it would be fun to watch everyone they know die? Did they think it would be fun to not know if you'd have enough food and water?"

"I don't know, sweetie," she said. "I think some people who weren't happy about-"

"Sarah!" he hissed, pointing toward something. "Look!"

Sarah followed the point of his finger toward a figure lying on the ground. The man was as dead as he could be, lying in a thick pool of rust-colored blood. Most of his head was missing, the result of its encounter with a large-caliber bullet. He was young, late teens, twenty at the most. He wore cargo shorts and a long-sleeve t-shirt, both were dark with blood stains.

Max screamed, the howl piercing the late-afternoon stillness, high-pitched, thin, a throwback to the pre-pubescent boy he'd been not too long ago. Sarah pulled Max close to her and clapped her left hand against his mouth. Then she unslung her M4 from her shoulder.

"Shhh."

The scream died in his throat, and he pressed up against her. Sarah scanned the area, keeping her finger tight on the trigger, but she detected no movement. Her head continued rotating in the silence. The tendons in her neck strained and popped as she did so.

She could feel Max's hot tears plopping on her arm, his whole body quivering with fear.

The second body was about fifty feet distant, the clothes soaked in blood. And beyond that, a third body. And a fourth. All butchered.

"THEY'RE ALL MEN," Sarah said after she'd conducted a quick search of the camp.

The wind had kicked up, the polyester skins of the tents flapping in the afternoon breeze. The tents had been arranged in a half-moon shape at the base of a hill, in the shade of a line of pines.

"So?" Freddie said.

"But there were at least two women with them."

"How do you figure?" Adam asked.

She waved him over with her right hand and led him from tent to tent.

"Four bodies, but there are six sleeping bags."

"How do you know there were women here?"

She cocked her head at him. Jesus, men could be so dense.

"Come here," she said. "Poke your head in this tent and take a whiff."

Adam complied with her request.

"You smell that?"

"What am I smelling for?"

"Jesus. Perfume."

"Oh yeah, now I smell it."

"Eternity," she said. "Calvin Klein. I used to wear it."

There were two backpacks in this tent, one containing women's clothing and other female personal effects. A wallet, black, leather and worn good, was tucked inside the pack. The driver's license inside had belonged to Patricia Williams, a resident of Indianapolis. The photograph hadn't done her much justice, if there was any to be done. Her hair was stringy, and a leathery face made her look ten years older than she was. But she seemed like a nice enough woman, certainly better than those who had unleashed the carnage in her camp.

"What happened?" Max asked, still rattled by the gruesomeness of the scene.

Sarah chewed on her lip as she thought about how to respond. On the one hand, Max was still a boy, still negotiating that shaky rope bridge between adolescence and manhood. On the other hand, circumstances now dictated he was going to have to grow up a lot faster than he might have otherwise. Sugarcoating things might backfire, make him feel like the world was safer than it really was. And it could seem safe now, what with going a day or two without even sniffing another human being. The sooner he understood the way the world worked, the better.

"I think the women in this camp were taken," she said.

"Taken?" Caroline repeated. "Taken where?"

Sarah shook her head, not wanting to give a voice to her darkest thoughts, about where these two women were right now, what they were enduring.

"Hey, look at this," Caroline called out.

Sarah followed Caroline's gaze, which was fixed on the side of a tent. A strange bit of graffiti had been spray-painted in black across the side of the tent. A silhouette of a large bird against an unidentifiable backdrop. Max thought the image looked like a set of sharp, pointy teeth, whereas Adam posited a roaring fire.

"Like a phoenix?" Freddie offered.

"Possibly."

Sarah felt a chill ripple through her. Bad enough they were traipsing through a human wasteland, eating canned goods, no idea what the future held for any of them. The dirt on the grave of the world still fresh, and already they're dealing with some kind of roaming death squad? This kind of thing was for shitty cable movies on Saturday afternoons.

She glanced at Adam, his arms crossed against his chest, his middle finger tapping against his bicep like a metronome. It was a pose she'd noticed him assume when he was deep in thought. The others had begun looking to him as the leader, even if Freddie had done so reluctantly. Guilt coursed through her, but that didn't mean she was sorry to transfer the weight of leadership to someone else's shoulders. It was the logical choice. Freddie was fixated on Caroline, who herself was busy with the business of healing and being pregnant. And she was a foot soldier. She took orders. Besides, who wanted to take orders from someone with a death wish? She glanced at Adam again.

Her conversation with Max replayed in her head. She hadn't been entirely honest with the boy. Yes, she had known soldiers who'd wished for an apocalypse. But she'd left out the part that she'd been one of them. It was so goddamn unfair, to know you were already dying at the age of thirty. To hear others talk about the future, about families, about careers, about this or that, when she was staring a death sentence in the face, it was enough to make anyone a little cuckoo. But the universe had seemed hell-bent on making her face her destiny, even as it had wiped the world clean of all those she'd once envied, the ones who had justifiably thought they had decades ahead of them, long, fruitful, more-or-less happy lives, those that now lay dead like abandoned toys.

THEY CAMPED six miles up the road. Adam had hoped

to get farther, but the group was exhausted, and Caroline had been complaining of severe back pain. It was an undeveloped parcel of land, clear-cut, easy to patrol. A pair of bulldozers sat at the edge of the property, waiting for drivers who would never be coming back to work. A large billboard reading *8 Acres Available NOW – Call Agent Bernice Sim!* stood at the edge of the tract.

Dinner was eaten in silence. No one wanted to cook, so they settled on protein bars and Gatorade. The discovery of the bodies had drained away what little life their merry little band had. Caroline was asleep within minutes of dinner's end, and Max joined her moments later. After dinner, Adam administered the last of the series of rabies shots. Well, he thought, as he depressed the plunger into his arm. That was that. The vaccine would either work or it wouldn't.

"We'll keep two on the perimeter all night," Adam said with as much authority as he could muster. "We'll stagger the shifts so that each of us can get a little sleep. Freddie, you stay here with these two."

Freddie nodded, the look in his eye of someone who had no intention of sleeping, and Adam and Sarah set out on the first shift. She gave him some pointers about using the gun as they circled the camp, but eventually, the conversation drifted off into silence. They walked quietly for a while. In the shadow of what they'd found earlier, everything seemed petty right now.

"Ask you a question?" Sarah asked.

"Sure."

"Let's say we find your daughter."

"Rachel."

"Right, Rachel. Say we find her."

"We'll find her!"

"Okay. But what then?"

"What do you mean?"

"What next?" she asked. "How do you spend the rest of your days?"

"I guess we do what anyone else left will do. Join up with other survivors. Find a safe place to live. Clean water. Food. I don't know. Maybe write a book."

She laughed at that, a light, infectious laugh that danced across the space between them and for a moment made him forget all the problems surrounding them, a broken world shattered into a million pieces. He glanced over at her, and saw a wide smile on her face. She wasn't looking at him, she wasn't really looking at anything. She just seemed to be enjoying the fact that she was enjoying something.

She ran a hand through her hair, tugging on the end of her jet-black locks, and a flash of sadness flickered across her face. She flipped her ponytail behind her back with authority, as though she'd caught herself engaging in childish thoughts, and the time for that was over.

"What?" he asked.

She shrugged.

"This might be the way things are for a while. We're gonna have to be extra careful."

"I realize that," he said.

"And, you know…" she said, her voice softening. "I just think it's important to stay realistic about what we're doing."

*She doesn't think we'll ever find her.*

They stood perfectly still, their eyes locking in the late-summer night. The silence was overwhelming, crushing, almost suffocating. Humanity's very existence had sported an ambient noise, a kind of radio static buzzing at the lowest threshold of one's attention, but now, with mankind scrubbed away like a chalkboard at the end of the school day, it was gone.

The look on his face must have given him away, told her he was bruising for an argument about it, readying his catalog of reasons why she was still alive, because she fell silent and resumed their patrol around the camp. He bit his tongue because he didn't want to make an impassioned argument totally devoid of objectivity only to realize a month from now that Sarah had been right all along, that Rachel was gone, vanished into the ether. Her surviving the plague was just one piece of the puzzle and that alone didn't mean he'd ever find her. Even if he made it to Tahoe in the next couple weeks, that didn't mean she would still be there. For all Rachel knew, he had died in the plague. And their link, the cell phones, was gone. Although he'd managed to charge his phone using a car adapter, it had been a week since he'd been able to draw any signal at all, rendering the device a useless brick.

These thoughts swirled about as Sarah continued her patrol, her head sweeping from side to side, using a flashlight to blow away the darkness. There was a hint of a chill in the air, nothing fierce really, but a coolness they hadn't felt yet in their time on the road. He didn't know much about this part of the country, particularly its late-summer weather patterns, and so he reminded himself they needed to start thinking about properly outfitting themselves for the elements.

He fell in step beside Sarah again.

"What do you think you'll miss the most?" she asked. "From before, I mean. Something you took for granted."

He thought about this for a moment, searching his memory banks for the things that had made the old world his own.

"There was a little barbecue place around the corner from where I lived," he said. "Ralph's, it was called. Made the best pulled pork sandwich I've ever had. They had this hot pepper vinegar. I probably ate there two, three times a week. Bring it home after work, sit on the couch. Slap your momma good."

"Excuse me?"

"You never heard that? Something so good it makes you want to slap your own mother?"

"Can't say that I have."

He looked at her and saw her smiling wistfully at his anecdote. Stupid as it was, he could see himself, weary after a long day at work, carrying a bag of greasy food into his house, plopping down at his old coffee table, eating his dinner while watching episodes of *Family Guy* he'd saved on his DVR. Now that he thought about it, he couldn't even remember the last time he had done it, and that pissed him off. Never had it been more apparent that he hadn't enjoyed the little things than in the face of their total disappearance.

"You?" he asked.

"Christmas," she said. "Christmas lights. I know people complained about how commercial everything had gotten, but it didn't bother me. I loved the sweaters and the decorations and the smell of Christmas dinner. I think being on duty a lot at Christmas made it easier to really like it. They tried to go all out for us when we were overseas."

"Well, I don't think commercialism at Christmas is going to be a problem this year."

"No. No, I guess not."

Her eyes shone in the moonlight, and he became conscious of how close they were standing. She was almost as tall as he was, maybe an inch shorter, and it was easy to stand there looking into her eyes, watching her chew on the corner of her lower lip when she was thinking about something, as he'd seen her do several times.

"Yeah," she said. "I think Christmas is the thing I will miss the most."

Adam leaned in and kissed her gently. Her lips tasted like the peppermint gum she chewed constantly. Every nerve ending in his body lit up, the kiss feeling new and fresh and yet like something he'd done a million times before. She leaned in, sliding her hand around the back of his head, their bodies pressed against one another, full of racing heat in a cold world of the lost and the dead, but she suddenly pulled away.

"I'm sorry," she said. "I can't."

"I, uh..." He started to say he was sorry, but that would have been a lie. He wasn't sorry.

"I, um..." she began, brushing her lips with a fingertip. "Maybe we split up for the rest of the shift."

He cleared his throat.

She looked down at her watch.

"Freddie's due to come on in an hour," she said. "I'm pretty wired, so you take the next break, and I'll take the one after that."

"You sure?"

"Yeah," she said.

He circled the perimeter for another hour, savoring the taste of her lips on his own, feeling somewhat stupid. Good job, Adam.

Freddie was awake when he went back to camp, sitting in the cone of light spilled by the LED lantern. Caroline and Max slept just beyond the shadows.

"You get some rest?" he asked the big man.

He nodded slowly, barely making eye contact with Adam. Adam unrolled his sleeping bag and slid in, feeling that anticipation of a good night's rest earned after a hard day.

"Are you OK?" he asked, propping himself up on his elbow.

"Fine," Freddie replied. He stood up and dusted off his legs. "Gun?"

Adam paused ever so slightly at the request, not long enough that Freddie noticed, but long enough that Adam wondered why he had done it at all. He handed the gun over to Freddie, the barrel pointing toward the ground like Sarah had taught them.

A yawn escaped Adam as Freddie joined Sarah on the watch. The two chatted briefly and then took up opposite positions on the imaginary circle surrounding the camp. After they fell into their respective patrols, Adam lay on his back and looked skyward. The stars were bright, burning their ancient fire millions of light years away, totally indifferent to the cataclysm that had enveloped this blue-green rock.

This is it now, he thought. This is the way things are. His little house on Floyd Avenue was empty, surrounded by other empty houses. The sidewalks were quiet, the bars and restaurants dark and stuffy and hot. School wouldn't be starting up this fall, no groan of yellow buses chugging through the neighborhoods. There would be no college football. No Halloween parties or pumpkin-spiced coffee or mall Christmas displays two months before anyone was ready to see them. It was all gone.

He was tired, but sleep wouldn't come. As much as Sarah's rejection had stung, it wasn't her she was thinking of. Instead, he found his thoughts swirling around Freddie Briggs. He still hadn't said much to anyone but Caroline; his devotion to her was nothing short of evangelical, the way a man might cleave to God after a miraculous experience. Adam didn't know if it was powered by love, dominance, obsession, duty, or some combination of the four. He seemed like a decent man, but Adam had been hoping they'd have made a deeper connection by now. They'd been on the road for days, and Adam knew nothing about him other than his name and that Caroline trusted him.

He lay awake for hours, thinking about the way he'd paused when Freddie had asked for the gun.

## 11

A few minutes before eight in the morning, Miles Chadwick entered the communal area of the *de facto* women's dormitory in the northwest corner of the compound. Tucked under his arm were the dossiers on the twelve women his hunting parties had rounded up in the previous week. Several cups of coffee sloshed around his stomach, but they had done little for the gumminess in his eyes. Sleep had eluded him again, as it had since they'd confirmed that Citadel women were infertile. He probably needed to try a sleeping pill, as he could feel the cloudiness increasing in his thinking process, an approaching cold front in his mind. He needed to be sharp, to make sure these women understood what their new roles were.

Twelve women.

He'd been hoping for twice that number, but the Citadel was, in some ways, a victim of its own morbid success. It had taken a lot longer than he'd anticipated to round up these twelve, let alone the two dozen he was hoping for, and they'd had to range out much farther from the compound. It was just more evidence of the totality of Medusa's work. Already, the hunting parties had drifted as far east as Illinois, north to Sioux Falls. Wichita to the south, west to the Nebraska/Colorado border. Some days, they wouldn't see a single survivor.

His orders had been simple. Find women of childbearing age and bring them back. Kill everyone else. This served to begin thinning the ranks of potential threats to the Citadel, albeit slowly, but then again, Rome hadn't been built in a day either. Ordering these executions pricked him with guilt, needling at him like a paper cut. Strange, really, given the fact he was guilty of murdering billions of people, but ordering the executions of Medusa survivors had seemed particularly barbaric to Chadwick. Simply by not succumbing to the virus, these folks had managed the nearly impossible, and here he was, having them murdered for the effort. Part of him wanted to bring them all in, part of the new regime building a new world from the ashes.

But he couldn't do that.

Control.

Everything had to be carefully controlled, especially in these early months and years. The future would depend on what they did now, the steps they took now. And introducing too many variables too soon could threaten everything.

Plus, there was the matter of protecting the Citadel's darkest secret.

He turned his thoughts back to their new captives.

The directive to capture women of child-bearing years had been, of course, open to some interpretation, and so the hunting parties had snared two young teenage girls in their patrols. Initially, Chadwick had not known what to do with them, but eventually, he'd had them blindfolded and dropped off a hundred miles away. So desperate for test subjects had he been that he had overlooked the potential benefit of bringing children into the Citadel fold. Maybe they'd start bringing in children in a few weeks. That it hadn't been discussed in the planning sessions of the Citadel high command made him feel a little stupid, and it made him think worriedly about what else they might have forgotten.

Because, as it turned out, it *had* been the vaccine that had rendered the original fifty women of the Citadel infertile. These twelve women were fertile, although one had had a pre-plague hysterectomy, and thus was of no use to Chadwick. He was still trying to decide what to do with her.

They were holding the women in a converted ware-house, which they had retrofitted with cheap walls to give them each their own room. Security at the ware-house was high, and he'd sedated the women. It wasn't the Waldorf-Astoria, but then again, these women were not guests here. It was important he reminded them of that, if only subtly. Quite frankly, these women were the Citadel's most important asset, whether they knew it or not, whether they wanted to admit it or not. But that meant expanding their footprint sooner than they had anticipated.

It was these women that would help usher in a new generation.

For the most part, they hadn't been too much trouble. Most were still in shock, either because of the cataclysm itself or by the manner in which they'd been taken. Some seemed happy to be here, enjoying the Citadel's hospitality, not asking any questions. And a couple of the women worried him.

It was the first time he'd seen all his new recruits assembled together. Several were crying softly. Eight Caucasian, two blacks, one Asian, one Latino. A fairly representative cross-section of the American female population before the epidemic. Their average age was thirty-four. All but one was under the age of forty, which he was particularly happy about. All had at least six or seven good years of fertility ahead of them, and Chadwick intended to take full advantage of every one of those. Two had refused to identify themselves, which annoyed him, but he really couldn't do anything about that. He needed them, and so they didn't realize the power they wielded. Yet. He needed to make sure they never figured that out. He wondered if any of them had figured out he was the one responsible for the end of the world.

He thumbed through each of the folders, scanning the names.

Marilyn Tate, 27 years old. Denver, Colorado.

Julie Micco, 37. Sioux City, Iowa.

Unidentified Caucasian woman, Mid-20s.

Nadia    Obeid,    34.    Stillwater,    Oklahoma. *(hysterectomy)*

Erin Thompson, 30. Des Moines, Iowa.

Robin Cobos, 33. Springfield, Missouri.

Patricia Williams, 44. Indianapolis, Indiana.

Sharee Hawkins, 34. Enid, Oklahoma.

Latasha Gilman, 28. Lincoln. Nebraska.

Kimberly Lockwood, 29. Sioux Falls, South Dakota.

Sasha Goodell, 34, St. Louis, Missouri.

Unidentified Chinese woman, Late 30s.

They were seated in a semi-circle in metal folding chairs, as though they were about to begin a group therapy session. Taking no chances, Chadwick had their ankles and wrists bound with zip ties, and two of his most trusted advisors patrolled the room with machine guns. He hadn't sedated them this morning, as he wanted them awake and alert. None of the women spoke.

He sat down in the empty chair and crossed one leg over the other.

"Good morning," he said, smiling broadly. "My name is Dr. Chadwick. I want to welcome you all to the Citadel."

"Where are we?" moaned one of them, her voice caked in sobs.

"Patricia, is it?"

She nodded, wiping her freely running nose with her bound wrists.

"This is your new home."

A stream of angry Chinese spewed from the Asian woman. She spoke no English, but tone was nothing if not universal. This triggered outbursts from the others, and Chadwick let them vent. Cutting them off would serve no purpose. Letting them get their say in would make them feel included, as though their opinion mattered. It didn't, of course, but they didn't need to know that.

The invective continued for another minute and then began to tail off.

"I'm happy to hear from each of you," he said. "But let's do this in a civilized manner. Ms. Williams, you were asking where we were."

She nodded. Patricia Williams was a short, slightly overweight woman with brown hair. When they found her, she'd been traveling with four men and an older woman; the group had not put up much of a fight. It would have been easy to attribute her forward question to a streak of self-confidence, but Chadwick didn't think that was the case. She struck him as impulsive, her mouth guided by sheer terror. She was a wonderful physical specimen for her age, her fertility tests belying a woman fifteen years younger.

"We're in a safe place," he said.

"What is this place?" asked Latasha Gilman.

"We're a group of scientists and engineers and doctors," he said. "This was a government installation. We're trying to build a completely self-sufficient society, off the grid. At least, we were trying to, before the outbreak."

"Why did you kill my friends?"

"My men felt like their lives were in danger."

Someone let loose a sarcastic laugh.

"How can so many of you still be alive?"

He paused for a moment, to maximize the dramatic effect of his response to the question.

"We had a vaccine."

Murmurs first, and then explosions, as he expected. A few broke down in tears.

"A vaccine?"

"You've gotta be kidding me!"

"They said there was no vaccine!"

He let them run for a bit and then used his hands

to calm them down, a conductor in his finest performance. The room was silent but for the continued weeping, as the women imagined what might have been. Children, husbands, sisters, brothers, all cut down when a simple shot in the arm might have saved them.

"There was a vaccine," he said. "Our government knew what this disease was."

"Why didn't they start mass vaccinations?" asked the unidentified white woman.

"They did," he lied. "On the east coast. Vaccinations had begun in New York and Boston, but the virus moved too quickly. I don't think they realized how quickly the disease would spread or how deadly it would be."

"How did you have the vaccine?" she asked.

"We have a number of vaccines here," Chadwick said, eyeing the woman carefully. "As I said, this installation was designed to be self-sufficient."

"How did you know to use that particular vaccine?" she asked. She was a pretty girl, a little heavyset perhaps. She wore glasses and kept her long brown hair tied in a ponytail.

"We did get lucky in that respect," he said, smiling at the question. "My medical director had some close friends at the Centers for Disease Control. They told him what was going on, that they knew they wouldn't be able to vaccinate enough people in time. That was in the middle of the first week of the outbreak. We began vaccinating everyone immediately and we simply had to hope the vaccine would take. We're in the middle of nowhere, no one coming in or out, so that bought us a little time. We circled the wagons, pulled up the drawbridge, and hoped for the best. Ten days later, our blood tests showed we all had antibodies to Medusa, and no one got sick. Just like you, the people here lost all their families, all their friends back home."

"Lucky you," the girl said, one eyebrow raised. Chadwick felt naked, exposed, as the girl looked at him, looked *through* him. He felt goosebumps erupt along his arms, but he held her gaze, intent on not being the first one to look away.

"No, my dear," Chadwick replied after she broke her gaze. "Lucky you. All of you. Immune to the greatest scourge that mankind has ever seen. All of you are miracles of evolution. Nature chose you to represent our species going forward."

"What do you want with us?" she asked, seemingly unimpressed with his praise of her DNA.

"Quite simply, we're trying to rebuild," he said. "This thing, it all but wiped us out. We've decided we need to start sooner than later if we don't want mankind to just fade away. It means working together, joining forces. It's a big world out there. If we leave it to chance, we may never get our old way of life back.

People will start to forget that we were once a great society, a great country."

"What if we want to leave?" Latasha Gilman asked.

"That's not going to be an option right now," he said as gently, as paternally, but as firmly as he could. There could be no misunderstanding about this. "Besides, you're much safer here than you are in the outside world."

The room fell silent for a moment. A chair creaked as one of the women shifted in her seat. He looked upon each woman in turn, holding each gaze like he was turning a key in a lock. Faces fell, jaws tightened, even more tears were shed, but this was quieter, more whimpering than weeping.

"Make no mistake, you will be cared for here," he said. "You have no idea how important you are."

He became acutely aware of the bespectacled girl eyeing him. Again, sweat trailed down the sides of his body. His voice began to crack.

"Thank you ladies. We'll be seeing a lot more of each other very soon. In the meantime, please enjoy your stay."

## 12

A dam spotted the UPS truck by the side of the road shortly before noon on September 18. They'd been walking along I-70 for nearly five days, taking turns pushing Caroline in the wheelchair. Out in the plains, farther and farther from the concentrated population centers, finding motorized transportation was becoming increasingly difficult, and with Caroline in her condition, bicycles were no longer an option. But that morning, just west of Topeka, Kansas, they'd found a big Ford Expedition, the keys in the ignition but its gas gauge tickling E, and a long stretch of empty road ahead. Adam cursed their luck. This big honker, with its seven seats, could make for some easy sledding out here, if they could only find some goddamn gas. So when he saw the boxy brown truck on the side of the road, a spike of relief shot through him.

"We'll siphon the gas out," Freddie had said after they'd pulled up behind the UPS truck.

"With what?"

"I've got a hose," he said.

And he hadn't been lying. A tightly spooled green coil of garden hose in his pack. For what, Adam had no earthly idea. But he had it, and maybe they could siphon the gas out of this UPS truck, if there was any to be had. It wasn't like they had any other options. If this didn't work, the Expedition would run dry, and they'd be walking along I-70, this big, empty gorgeous stretch of road, with no wheels.

*Water, water, everywhere, not a drop to drink.*

As Adam stepped down to the pavement, he felt a cool breeze rustle his shirt. The rain they'd awoken to had pushed off, leaving behind a clear, sunsplashed afternoon. Fall. That first taste of it right at summer's end. Just a little taste. It was hard to picture the seasons changing with so much of his subconscious still occupied by those hot, hellish, plague-ridden days of August. But ended they had, just like summer would. The world was going to keep right on spinning, with or without them.

Adam and Sarah scouted out the UPS truck, but all they found was the desiccated corpse of the driver in the front seat, still wearing the familiar brown uniform. Here was a case study in Medusa. Guy wakes up, feeling a little off, heads off to work anyway. Delivers packages and death. A few hours later, the virus ravaging him now, he pulls off the road for a quick nap. Closes his eyes and that was that.

"Clear," Sarah called out, and Freddie got to work on the gasoline.

"How long has it been since the outbreak?" Sarah asked as she watched Freddie feed the tank of the SUV.

Adam checked his watch.

"Today's September 18," he said. "Five, six weeks."

"So call it a month since everything broke down?"

"Sounds about right," Adam said. "Why do you ask?"

"The gasoline. It's going to go over soon."

"What?" Freddie asked, looking back over his shoulder.

Adam blew out a noisy sigh.

"She's right," Adam said. "Gasoline goes bad. The stuff with ethanol, that's got a shelf life of about three months or four months."

"Jesus H. Christ," Freddie said. "Ain't we ever gonna catch a break?"

Adam rubbed his eyes and chuckled to himself.

"We'll figure something out," he said.

"Hey, check this out!" Max called out, his exuberance cutting through the sudden frost like hot steel.

Sarah followed Max's voice to the back of the UPS truck, where she found the kid climbing into the open cargo bay. She peeked around him and saw dozens of packages still in the truck.

"It's like Christmas!" Max shouted as he began digging through the boxes.

Although it seemed a bit morbid, Sarah couldn't help but smile a little as the boy pawed through the packages.

"Go on and bring them out here," Adam said. "We'll load them up and go through them when we make camp tonight."

Max jumped on his new assignment, quickly clearing the truck of sixty-five boxes and envelopes. He created three piles: small, medium and large.

"Can I open them now?" Max asked when he'd finished.

Adam checked his watch, his eyes narrowing. Sarah could tell he wanted to go, go, go, narrow the gap between him and his daughter.

"OK," he said. "We'll take an hour to go through them. It's one-twenty now. I want to be back on the road by two-thirty."

Max's face lit up.

"You open," Adam said, "and I'll keep a list. Deal?"

Sarah felt her stomach flip with excitement as Max nodded.

They found a notepad and pen in the glove compartment, and Max set to work tearing open the packages and envelopes. Before opening each one, he read the name and address of the package's intended recipient. It felt weird and awkward at the beginning, but after half a dozen or so, Sarah was glad Max was doing it. In some small way, it felt like a memorial service for these sixty-five people they'd never met, who almost certainly lay dead in a hospital or bedroom or in a shallow grave and would otherwise have been lost to history.

The names flowed through them like a dark, deep river, rich with hidden meaning and import, but rushing by too quickly to impart any truth.

"Natalie Sears. 543 Michigan Avenue. Yukon, Pennsylvania."

A prom dress.

"Russell Yang. 3231 Godfrey Street. Salem, Oregon."

A case of printer paper.

The unboxing revealed a dizzying array of treasures, from gourmet coffee to a real estate sales contract, a Polaroid camera to a purple vibrator (and hadn't *that* been a fun one to explain to Max), a cashmere scarf to a collection of dog toys. Cans of Campbell soup and a traffic cone. A set of car keys attached to a University of Missouri keychain. A jar of gourmet peanuts. A portable video game system. A hardcover novel. A sheaf of multi-colored construction paper bearing finger-paints of little hands and glued-on pipe cleaners. X-rays. DVDs of old movies. Deeper they dug into the scores of dead letters and deeper ran the fissures in Sarah's heart, until it was on the verge of breaking. America. This was America they were opening, one piece at a time, an America that had disappeared around them like a mirage.

It was well past two-thirty when they finally finished, but no one seemed to care that they'd missed their self-imposed deadline. As she wiped tears from her face, Sarah looked up to see Freddie doing the same thing. And after all that, only a handful of boxes contained anything worth taking. The soup. The garlic peanuts. A carton of cigarettes. A novel called *The Poacher's Son* that Max wanted to take.

God *damn*, this was hard, she thought. God damn.

Maybe they'd needed this. Her last memories of the old world were of it sick, dying and panicky, caught in a humiliating pose. The looting and the riots and the fear. The Bronx. She combed her memory banks for something before the plague. An early outbreak of flu, she'd heard on the news.

*Before that, though, Wells, before that. Something before that.*

St. Croix, back in March. She and two of her girlfriends, Keri Williams and Dawn Vann, officers like she'd been, now dead like she wasn't, had bugged out to St. Croix for three days, drank and flirted and she hooked up with one guy, an architect from San Diego, if she remembered right. A quickie in the hallway outside her room, and thank God she'd had a condom with her because she was going to bang him whether she'd had one or not. It had been a fun trip, the last fun thing she remembered doing because then she was working a lot, getting ready to ship out in September. She supposed she felt a little better and, as she looked around at the other faces, she suspected her friends might have been engaging in similar trips down memory lane.

They tossed the white elephants back in the truck and shut the cargo doors. As Sarah stepped on to the running board to slip behind the wheel of the Expedition, she caught movement in the corner of her eye. She turned toward it, toward the dead cornfields to the north, and saw a lone figure staggering toward them.

Sarah and Adam raised their weapons as the figure approached, but the straggler either didn't see them or didn't care, and collapsed at the edge of the cornfield. With Adam covering her, Sarah approached the figure, a woman, she could see now. She was olive-skinned, her eyes a fierce green color but clouded with confusion and fatigue. She was ranting, her words coming in a machine-gun spray of English and Arabic.

"My God," Caroline said to no one.

She was filthy, barefoot and dressed in tattered blue coveralls. Her arms and feet had been scratched and scraped to hell, and she was woefully thin. Her cheeks were sunken in, and her eyes were glassy. When Adam knelt to examine her, she recoiled away from him, violently, and toward Sarah. He backed away from her, his hands up in surrender. She seemed to relax, if only a hair, as Sarah tried to soothe her.

"Hey there, you're gonna be OK," Sarah said. "You're gonna be OK."

She repeated it over and over.

"Get me some water for her," Sarah ordered.

Max brought two bottles and a hunk of bread to Sarah, who handed them over to the woman. Even Max seemed to understand that Sarah would be this woman's intermediary for the time being. She guzzled both bottles of water and ate the food so quickly that Adam worried she might choke on it.

When she was done, Sarah took the woman's hand in her own.

"Sarah, look at her arm," Adam said.

Sarah gently turned the woman's wrist and gasped. Burned into the underside of her wrist was a tattoo. It was the same phoenix rising from the ashes they'd seen spray-painted on the tent earlier. The woman looked at her, the panic bubbling on her face like a pot of water left unattended.

"It's okay," Sarah said. "You're safe now. We're all together."

The woman swung her head toward Adam and then back to Sarah, as though she were trying to decide whether to believe them.

"Sarah, a word?" Adam said.

They stepped away from the group.

"She's been hurt bad," he said to Sarah. "Possibly raped. Make sure she knows it's her decision."

"What if she says no?" Sarah replied. "I won't leave her alone."

"She won't say no," Adam said, although he really had no idea what the woman would do.

Sarah and Caroline went back and sat next to the woman on the ground; Adam motioned for the men, and the three of them drifted down the highway to give the women some privacy. They stood awkwardly, shifting their weight from foot to foot. Max, who was short for his age, looked up at them like a child caught between warring parents.

He watched Sarah console the woman, who'd burst into tears once she was with Caroline and Sarah. She buried her face into Sarah's shoulder and wailed, the sound almost painful to hear. It was as though all the grief that had accumulated since the outbreak was flooding out in one fell swoop, as though she'd never had a chance to deal with what had happened. Sarah and Caroline sat with her, holding her hand as the woman slowly regained her bearings. Her voice softened, her herky-jerky movements slowed down. As they waited, he found himself hoping very much that the woman would come with them. Sure, he wanted the woman to be safe. If she could find comfort in their ragtag group, so be it. But that wasn't the whole story. He stole glances at Sarah's face, at the angled cheekbone, at the eyes that glimmered in the light. He liked the way her t-shirt fit her body, the slender sheath of muscle in each of her arms.

The kiss they'd shared hadn't been far from his mind. There had been something there, he was sure of it. They hadn't discussed it, but in the past week, he'd caught her staring at him the way she'd caught him eyeing her. But she had remained silent. And, he supposed, maybe there just wasn't any room on their plate for that kind of nonsense right now.

"I hope your daughter is still alive," Freddie said, jarring Adam from his daydream.

"Oh," Adam replied. "Thanks. I'm not kidding myself. I know it's a long shot."

"I'll be honest with you," Freddie said, his voice dropping to a whisper. "I saw both my girls die, and I don't know what's worse. Knowing they're gone forever or not knowing at all."

Adam couldn't imagine anything worse than knowing Rachel was dead, but in a perverse sort of way, he understood what Freddie meant. What if he were just setting himself up for crushing disappointment? What if he never found her? Wouldn't that be worse than just knowing that she was dead? These questions spun through his head like a hamster on a wheel, haunting him as Sarah and Caroline counseled the woman. He tried to think of something else, anything else, but out here, in the big nowhere, there was nothing else to think about.

"I'm very sorry about your family," Adam said.

"What can you do?" Freddie replied. "Some of us just draw the shitty hand."

Adam didn't know how to reply. He wasn't sure if Freddie was just firing off platitudes or if that last comment had been a dig aimed at him.

"It's a terrible thing," Adam said.

An hour later, Sarah and Caroline approached Adam, Freddie, and Max, the newcomer hanging well behind them.

"Guys, this is Nadia," Sarah said.

"Nadia, this is Adam, Freddie and Max."

Adam and Freddie nodded.

"Hi," Max said.

Nadia nodded toward Max, but she didn't make eye contact with Freddie or Adam.

"Nadia has agreed to join us," she said.

Nadia nodded again.

Caroline took Nadia's hand in her own and squeezed it. Nadia placed her hand against Caroline's swollen belly and smiled. They loaded up the Expedition, and ten minutes later, they were westbound again.

*What if?*

*What if?*

*What if?*

## 13

"**A**dam."

He whimpered softly.

"Adam," Freddie repeated again, this time shaking his shoulder. "Wake up, man."

He didn't want to. His head throbbed and, along with the dry, gummed-up mouth, foretold the hangover that awaited him. And being shaken awake wasn't helping. Whatever it was would have to wait. But then Freddie said the one thing that made him forget about the hangover, about the headache, the one thing that terrified him above all else.

"Baby's sick."

Adam sat up like a shot, sending his systems into massive revolt. His head swam, conspiring with his stomach to magnify the nausea tenfold, and then there was nothing he could do to stop it. He scampered out of his sleeping bag as far as he could before his insides erupted. On his hands and knees, gripping the dirt for dear life, he waited as his body violently flushed out the remains of the previous day's festivities, Freddie's terrible message pinging away in his brain.

Freddie handed him a bottle of water, and Adam drank it down. It was lukewarm, but that was fine by him. Made it go down a little faster, without the threat of brain freeze. His desiccated body absorbed the water like a new sponge. He used a bit of the water to wash out his mouth, and then he wiped his lips clean with the back of his sleeve.

*Baby's sick.*

The words were like bullets to the chest.

*God dammit, why had he let himself get his hopes up?*

After taking a deep breath, he staggered to his feet and followed Freddie toward Caroline's tent. A light but steady rain was falling from low, gray clouds, which were nestled in the kind of sky that told you you'd be better off just staying in bed and watching movies. The rain rustled the leaves, spattering the shells of their polyester tents, steady, steady, steady. They were a few miles east of Salina, Kansas, where, on September 20, they'd set up their most permanent home to date, waiting for the baby to come. Adam hated to stop their progress, but the travel was starting to wear on Caroline. Plus, his last examination of her suggested the baby had dropped and would be coming any moment.

Caroline had gone into labor early on the morning of September 26. By the early afternoon, her contractions were four minutes apart, and she couldn't wait any longer. With Sarah and Freddie working as *de facto* nurses, Adam set about the familiar work of bringing new life to the world, even if it was into a world with which he was decidedly unfamiliar. It had been a smooth delivery, given the circumstances. Caroline had told him her original birth plan had been to deliver without pain medication (and Adam couldn't help but smile, virtually all of them said that, and then virtually all of them accepted the epidural after one or two good contractions). In this case, however, Caroline had gotten her wish. Oh, she had most certainly gotten her wish.

And six hours after she started pushing, right about the time he'd started thinking about an emergency C-section, out came a healthy, howling baby boy, out the way they had come for the entire history of the human race, his skin as fair as his mother's, his head topped with a fine layer of red fuzz. He maxed out the 1-minute and 5-minute Apgar scores, pinking up and screaming his little head off. It was the most beautiful thing Adam had ever seen, and in that moment, as he handed the infant to his exhausted mother, all their problems just fell away. She named him Stephen, in honor of his father, who had succumbed in the second week of the epidemic. Their good luck continued several hours after his birth, when he began nursing like a seasoned professional.

They passed the baby around like a good joint, each taking a hit of that baby smell, and even Freddie seemed happy. He made ga-ga faces and changed diapers so Caroline could sleep in between feedings. Thirty-six hours in, Adam had started to relax, enjoying a cigar and a scotch while the others passed around a bottle of champagne Sarah had snagged during a supply run. The baby was feeding well, sleeping in two to three-hour bursts. He'd even found his thumb and was happy and alert.

One scotch became four, and on no sleep since Caroline had gone into labor, the alcohol had hit him hard and fast, precipitating the hangover he was feeling as he hurried into Caroline's tent. He found her tucked in her sleeping bag, holding the baby close to her body.

Stephen was coughing, those tiny hacks, and immediately, Adam tried to attribute it to anything but what he feared it would be. Allergies. Drool. Milk going down the wrong pipe. He always thought it funny that doctors did the same thing as their patients, their minds working the same way, to explain away the thing that you feared the most.

"When did this start?" Adam said, kneeling by her.

She looked exhausted, and the glow that had been there after Stephen's arrival had faded badly, like a once shiny penny that had been put through its paces.

"About two hours ago," she said. "And I think he's running a fever."

A soft hand to Stephen's fragile forehead confirmed Caroline's diagnosis. The tiny little boy, a wrinkly, squirmy pile of pink, was wearing nothing but a diaper, but he was still warm, very warm. Adam wrapped his hands around the boy's toothpick legs and found those uncomfortably warm as well.

Adam fought to maintain as straight a face as he could. In normal circumstances, a fever in an infant under twelve weeks of age was deadly serious, warranting immediate medical intervention. Hearing it now made him weak, dizzy, and if he hadn't had one knee firmly planted in the ground, he might have tumbled over.

"I don't want to jump to any conclusions," Adam began, "but I'm not going to lie to you. This is not what I was hoping to see."

Her jaw clenched tight, and he saw the panic bubbling there like a forgotten pot of soup, her eyes bouncing from Adam to Freddie and back again. She stared at him, and he could feel it in her stare.

"Do something!" Freddie barked.

A cough, a deeper one, exploded from Stephen's

little chest, and Caroline continued to rock him as she began to cry.

"Jesus!" Freddie snapped. He pointed at Adam. "You. Outside."

Adam recoiled as a spike of fear coursed through him.

"Be right back," Freddie said, but Caroline wasn't listening. She rocked Stephen gently in her arms as the men ducked through the flaps of the tent.

Outside, the rain had intensified. Sarah and Max were lingering by the tent, anxious to hold the baby, anxious to kiss the baby, anxious to just be in the same goddamn room with the baby. They were like addicts waiting for their dealer to dish out a little more of that sweet, sweet horse.

"God dammit, ain't there anything you can do?" Freddie asked.

"What's wrong?" Sarah asked.

"Stephen's sick."

"Aw, shit."

"No, no, no!" Max said, bursting into tears.

"Is there anything you can try?" Sarah asked.

"I don't know what I can do," Adam said. "Not if he's got it."

"What the hell kind of doctor are you?" Freddie snapped. His cheeks flushed, his left eyebrow twitching.

"A realistic one," Adam said. "I don't want to get her hopes up."

"There's got to be something."

"You've seen what it does," Adam said.

Max fled back to his tent, leaving the three of them standing there in the rain. Freddie closed his eyes, his breathing shallow and ragged. He placed his massive hand on Adam's chest.

"Please," he said, his eyes closed now. "Can you just try?"

"How about we leave the doctor stuff to me? How about that?"

Freddie's face drained of color, Adam's emasculation reaching him at his very core. Adam hadn't set out to embarrass the man, but he had to take control of the situation. If his expertise, the one thing he brought to the table, was going to mean anything, he had to plant his flag now.

Freddie stormed back inside the tent. Just like that, Adam and Sarah were alone again.

"You really think he's got it?"

Adam looked down at his shoes.

"Maybe it's just a cold or something," Sarah said.

"I don't think so."

"These aren't exactly ideal conditions," she said. "Maybe he picked up something on the road. I just don't want to assume all is lost."

They stood in silence, and he watched her

watching him, wondering if she now regretted hitching her wagon to his, wondering if he wasn't the man she had thought he was.

"I can try an antiviral," he said finally. "I heard some chatter it was distantly related to the influenza virus, but I have no idea if that's accurate. It's not usually indicated for infants this young, but there isn't really any other option. Maybe a combination of the medicine and any antibodies he inherited from her will make a difference."

"OK. An antiviral. Can we find it in a pharmacy?"

"Yes. Assuming there are any supplies left. Remember, I'm sure everyone and their brother tried it during the outbreak."

"You always this glass-is-half-empty?"

"Can you blame me?"

"No, I guess not."

She turned toward the tent's opening, and he grabbed her gently by the wrist.

"Seriously," he said as she turned back to face him. "Please don't get her hopes up. I'm telling you this as a doctor. This is a Hail Mary pass."

THEY POWERED WEST ALL MORNING, hitting half a dozen pharmacies, unable to find antivirals, unable to find virtually any medicine at all. At noon, they reached the outskirts of Salina, smack in the dead center of Kansas. Salina had been at the hub of the state's wheat industry, once a pleasant city of about fifty thousand souls. In the eastern suburbs, where Adam and Sarah had found a Walgreen's drug store, cookie cutter development had been in full swing when the plague had hit, giving them a sense of the familiar they'd seen in almost every town and city they'd passed through on their trek west.

The box-shaped building was at the south end of a strip mall, bordering a new residential neighborhood. The moisture barriers for half-completed homes flapped in the rain, the skeletal shells of the unfinished homes beginning to bear the scars of inattention. New saplings dotted the area, but the once-manicured common areas were starting to go to seed. An Applebee's restaurant anchored the shopping center, the words IMMEDIATE SEATING AVAILABLE still flashing in the window, a gaudy, neon red. This gave Adam the willies almost more than anything they'd seen on the road.

"Power's on here," he said, pointing toward the restaurant.

"Strange," she said.

"Backup generators?"

"I suppose."

Sarah glassed the area with a pair or binoculars, shaking her head after a moment.

"I don't know about this one," Adam said. "Maybe we should keep looking."

"Didn't you say time is of the essence?"

"Yes," he said. "Every minute counts with an antiviral. The longer we wait, the less effective it will be."

"Then we go in here. You got your piece?"

He nodded.

"You sure you're ready to use it?"

He nodded firmly, hoping it masked his terror.

He cleared the chamber and made sure the pistol was ready to fire as Sarah swung the doors open.

"Ready?"

He nodded, his face oily with sweat. It was cool out, still drizzling, but his cheeks were hot, and perspiration matted his shirt to his skin.

"Stay behind me," she said.

Adam's heart was pounding as they crossed the threshold into the store, which was silent but for the buzz of the overhead lights. Sarah motioned skyward toward a closed-circuit television mounted near the ceiling, still functioning. The picture cycled from one angle of the store to the next, giving clear views of each aisle. The store appeared empty, but Sarah maintained her position, crouched over, her hands gripped tight around her weapon.

"Stay alert," she whispered, her face taut, her jaw set like stone.

Using the long shelves for cover, they moved from

aisle to aisle, poking their heads around ransacked displays of sunscreen, disposable cameras and corn chips. After they finished their sweep, Sarah led him back to the middle of the store, and they moved in tandem down the center aisle, back to back. The place was a mess, the shelves stripped bare, disheveled, toys and tchotchkes littering the linoleum floor. An issue of *People* lay face up on the floor, a pair of married celebrities adorning the cover. The headline read, *More Kids for Hollywood's Power Couple?* It was dated August 6, a harsh reminder of how quickly the world had ended. As they moved deeper into the store, Adam began to lose hope, as the place had been picked over pretty well.

The pharmacy, which was at the back of the store, was dark, the overhead lights shattered. Bits of glass littered the floor, crunching under their feet as Adam checked the shelves. There wasn't much left. Bulk containers holding pills to treat high blood pressure, high cholesterol, and erectile dysfunction lined the shelves, but the antibiotics and narcotics were gone. He was about to give up hope when two stray bottles on a nearly bare shelf caught his eye.

*Please, please*, he thought.

He grabbed one of the bottles and studied the label.

Oseltamivir phosphate.

*The antiviral.*

It was the generic form, with nothing on the label to indicate that it was an antiviral. It was in capsule form, so they'd have to crush the contents into a bottle of formula for him. He still didn't think it was going to work, but at least they were doing something. And he owed that to Caroline. To let her know he had done all he could.

"I've got it," he called out.

When Sarah didn't reply, he froze. He leaned back, staying in shadow, and peeked out toward the store proper. From his vantage point, he could just make out Sarah's profile. Behind her, a slender arm, holding a gun to the back of her head.

He looked around and saw a closed-circuit monitor mounted on the counter. The black-and-white picture flickered through two shots of the store before snapping over to the pharmacy area. In the three seconds the shot remained on screen, Adam picked out two bandits, a skinny man and a heavier-set woman, both young.

"Come out with your hands up," a gruff voice called out. "Gonna count to three. Then the bitch gets it."

*Bitch.*

Well, he thought, at least that told him what kind of folks he was dealing with here.

"You hear me?" the man barked, his voice screeching now.

Adam chewed on his lip, the edges of a plan taking shape in his mind. He pulled the gun from his waistband and considered his options. He stared at the gun like it was an alien artifact, beyond the powers of his puny human comprehension. One versus two. And Sarah was being held hostage. In his untrained hands, the gun would be about as useful as a ball of yarn.

"I'm coming out!" he said, setting the gun and the antiviral down. He scanned the shelves and grabbed two more bottles.

*Oh, Adam, what the hell are you doing, buddy?*

He eased his way around the counter and out into the aisle fronting the pharmacy, his hands sky high, the pill bottles visible in his partially clenched fist. Sarah was about six feet away, a girl close in behind her, the gun pressed firmly against her temple. The girl's face was blank, betraying not a single emotion. She was heavier set, her hair cut short. The second gunman, whose wide face and even wider-set eyes reminded Adam of an owl, stood just off their shoulder, brandishing a shotgun. Sarah's M4 hung from his shoulder. He aimed the shotgun directly at Adam's face. The twin bores, black and empty, stared at Adam like a dead-eyed monster.

"What's in your hand?" the owl said, his words marinated with a thick Southern accent.

"Medicine."

"What for?"

"You promise to let us go if I tell you?" Adam asked.

"How about you give it to me 'fore I kill you?" Owl snapped.

"If you kill me, you won't know how to use it."

"What's it for?"

The temperature seemed to be climbing with each passing moment. Adam felt rivulets of sweat channeling down his sides, and he tried to steady his breathing.

"It."

An audible gasp.

"You mean *Snake*?" the girl said.

Snake. Medusa. So many names. Adam nodded as gravely as he could.

"That shit's gone," the girl snapped, her words clipped and desperate. "Everyone left's 'mune."

"Lucy, he's just bullshitting you," the owl said.

"Yeah, we thought everyone was immune, too," Adam said, gently lowering his hands to his head. It was a calculated risk, but he thought if he kept his hands over his head, they wouldn't notice. Especially given the bomb he was about to drop on them. His arms were starting to burn; it was time to play his hand. He held his final card, holding, holding, as he watched their jaws tighten, their eyes widen with fear.

"Until she came down with it yesterday," he said, jutting his chin directly toward Sarah.

Lucy's deep-seated instinct to survive kicked in, and

she shoved Sarah away from her hard, stumbling backwards as she did so. Sarah lost her own footing, crashing into Adam and sending them both to the ground. Owl was on the retreat now too, holding his hand up, as if that might stop the spread of the phantom illness. Lucy was wiping her hands down on her jeans, pulling her shirt collar up over her lips and nose.

"No, no," Owl said. He raised the gun back up and covered his mouth with his sleeve.

"No, wait!" Adam said. "If you shoot her, you'll spray blood everywhere. Then you'll definitely be exposed. There's still time. She hasn't coughed or sneezed since we came inside the store!"

"What?" Lucy said.

"I'm a doctor, trust me!" Adam said. "Medusa spreads like the common cold. You have to be exposed to droplets of the virus. You can't get it otherwise."

"You're shitting me!" Owl said.

"No, I was with a CDC team in Kansas City during the outbreak," Adam lied. "We figured out that the disease spreads easily, but not that easily. But you gotta get out of here now!"

The owl stood there, shifting his weight from foot to foot.

"Jack, let's go!" cried Lucy. "I fucking touched her!"

"Go on now," Adam said as grimly as he could. "Before it's too late. She's been coughing and sneezing a lot. I can't believe she hasn't yet in the store."

"What about you?" Jack asked.

Adam shook his head.

Jack's finger slipped in and out of the trigger guard as he swung from one choice to the other. Murder or flight.

"Please, hurry," Adam yelled. "Please, I don't want you all to get sick!"

"What about the medicine?" Owl asked. "It won't work. If it worked, everyone would still be alive."

"This medicine works," Adam said. "They just didn't have enough of it. I found some hidden in the back. This is the last of it."

"Give it to me!" he said.

Adam gingerly handed the bottles to the man, as though the very act of it pained him. As Jack took the bottles, Sarah's M4 slid off his shoulder and clattered to the tile floor. But Jack left it there and fled down the aisle.

"Jackie, wait!" shouted Lucy, pursuing her companion.

"Stay away from me!" he called out, his panic-filled voice echoing through the nearly empty drugstore. "Don't you come near me!"

Their howls continued out the door into the parking lot; eventually they drifted away, leaving Adam and Sarah alone in the store. Adam placed his hands on his knees and took some deep breaths; he felt dizzy and hot.

"Jesus Christ," he said. "I thought we were dead."

"Wow," Sarah said, retrieving her M4. "Where did you come up with that?"

"I don't know," he said. "I knew I had no chance with the gun. Then it occurred to me that if there's one thing everyone's still afraid of, it's Medusa. Wait here."

"Where are you going?"

"I gave him blood pressure medication. The antiviral is still in the back."

Sarah laughed out loud.

Adam retrieved the bottles from the pharmacy, and they left the store. The rain had stopped, but it was still cloudy and misty. He threw the truck into drive and screeched out of the parking lot.

## 14

They buried baby Stephen in the shade of a large pine tree on the edge of the camp.

Deep down, he'd known there was nothing they'd be able to do, that the trip he'd taken with Sarah had been nothing more than a lark and frolic, one that had nearly gotten them killed. They'd fought the good fight, administering as much medicine as they could, as often as they could. It had given Caroline a small measure of comfort, there at the end, as Stephen drew his last few breaths. But in the end, it hadn't done any good. His fever continued climbing, the cough worsening and deepening. And, as Adam expected, Medusa did to Stephen what it had done to everyone else, and he had died on the morning of September 30.

"Thank you for trying," she'd said to Adam,

holding Stephen close to her, quiet and free of his suffering.

Freddie spent the afternoon digging a tiny grave for Stephen. He took great care in doing so, excavating a small but virtually perfect rectangle that faced east. Caroline liked that it looked back across the empty country toward Georgia, where, in another life, another universe, another dimension, little Stephen would have grown up.

The women stood at the foot of the grave; Caroline wept silently, her left arm linked in Sarah's, her right in Nadia's. Max stood next to Adam, shifting his weight from one foot to the other, silent, miserable. At Caroline's request, Adam held Stephen and would be the one to hand him over to Freddie for his final interment.

"Can I touch him one more time?" Caroline asked, looking over at Adam.

He didn't know why she thought she had to ask, but he looked into her pleading eyes, flowing with tears, and it seemed important to her that he bless her request.

He nodded.

Stephen's body was wrapped in a light blue baby blanket, peppered with all manner of airplanes and helicopters and spaceships, which Caroline had been carrying with her for weeks. It had become a talisman in the last days of her pregnancy, but now, instead of naptimes and comfort, this blanket would serve as his shroud. She took him into her arms, held him close and kissed him on the head. Adam wondered if she would uncover his face, and he hoped she wouldn't. See, in her mind, she was picturing the face she'd seen upon his birth, the face she'd imagined a million times as an expectant mommy. To look at his face now, in the aftermath of its terrible war with Medusa, would destroy that and remind her of all that was awful and dark and evil.

But she did.

She unwrapped the blanket and kissed his forehead and his cheeks, and she began to wail. Adam closed his eyes and waited for it to be over.

"It's time to say goodbye," he heard Sarah say.

He opened his eyes and saw Sarah holding Caroline's face, red and gaunt, in her hands. He thought she did this to discourage her from kissing the baby again.

"It's time to say goodbye," Sarah said again.

Caroline nodded and passed the baby to Freddie, who lay Stephen down on the black dirt, so tiny and small, given back to the world that hadn't given him anything, not even a chance. The big man knelt down and picked a few stray bits of dirt off the blanket, an act of kindness that Adam found almost incomprehensibly sad.

"Adam?" Caroline asked, her face still in Sarah's hands.

He looked at her.

"Would you say something?" she asked. "For Stephen."

She looked at him again, with that expectant face, the one that had once looked upon him with hope and promise and belief that it was all going to work out, because seriously, what were the odds that she'd find an obstetrician after *ALL THIS*?

"Of course," he said, his words barely a whisper.

He cleared his throat and searched for something to say, anything to give this poor woman comfort. Any of them, really. He looked down at the small figure, free of all the horrors this world had seen fit to share with them.

"Dear Lord, we gather here today to say goodbye to a very brave, very beautiful little boy."

Caroline began to sob.

"This world we live in now, it's a new world for all of us."

He paused, the words not coming easily. He didn't know if he was coming across as sincere. He didn't know if this was comforting Caroline or torturing her. They were just words. What good could these stupid words do? No matter how beautifully or eloquently he spoke, Stephen would still be dead. The world would still be a graveyard. But he pressed onward, aware of his voice, his posture, everything feeling wrong, wrong, wrong.

"And I don't know why You chose to take him back so soon after he got here. But, I suppose, that may not be for us to know. So, all we can ask is that You welcome baby Stephen into Your loving arms. That You look after him now and always. That You bring his mother comfort and solace for the difficult days ahead. That You protect us and give us the guidance and wisdom we will need going forward.

"Amen."

A ripple of *Amens* from the others.

They all looked at Caroline, who continued staring down into her son's grave.

"Thank you, Adam," she said. "That was very nice."

She said it flatly, without emotion. Adam felt like she was just going through the paces, saying the things she thought people would expect her to say.

Each of them carefully poured a shovelful of dirt into the grave, Caroline going last. She sprinkled the dirt gently over her son and handed the shovel back to Freddie. As Freddie refilled the hole with the loose dirt, Caroline drifted away from the group, away to deal with her grief however she planned to deal with it. Adam, Sarah, Nadia, and Max watched as the dirt piled up, up, up until the hole was full.

THE SCOTCH TASTED DIFFERENT.

What had been warm and inviting on the day Stephen had been born, like a roaring fire on a cold New England night, now tasted swampy and hot. It reminded Adam of all those houses under gunmetal skies in all those towns and cities they'd passed through, the air conditioning long dead, full of roasting corpses.

But Adam drank it just the same. He tipped the bottle to his mouth, feeling it scorch its way down like gasoline, and nestled the bottle between his thighs. He was seated on the floor of his tent, at the foot of his sleeping bag, exhausted but awake. It was late, after midnight. Fast-moving clouds zipped along overhead, giving a slight strobe effect to the night.

As a clinical matter, he knew he was drunk. If he'd been out driving and had been pulled over by an observant state trooper (and what he wouldn't have given to see a cruiser blow by on a busy highway, its blue lights oscillating, pulsing with tremendous urgency and importance), he'd blow right past the limit just as simple as you please. But he didn't feel drunk. He didn't feel anything. Whatever the opposite of feeling was, that's what it was. He suspected it might have been within shouting distance of what Caroline was feeling.

Sure, the world had ended, had come undone around him like a sandcastle at high tide, but even then he'd felt something. *Terror. Panic. Confusion.*

Those were all full-blooded feelings. And then he'd heard the message from Rachel, and that had been another feeling. *Joy. Relief.* So there, the gamut of human emotion was still there, even at the end of all things.

But this. This was something else.

An absence of emotion. Numbness. The way your lips feel after the Novocaine.

How easy it had been to say the words at Stephen's memorial, to make them sound good. He'd never enjoyed laying down words of comfort when a patient had lost a pregnancy or the Pap smear had come back abnormal, but they seemed to work. And so he had done it, without believing the words he was saying, the way he hadn't believed the words he was uttering at Stephen's funeral.

After the memorial, each of them had retreated from the gravesite into his or her own tent, forsaking the group dinner. No one felt like eating anyway. As night had fallen, the camp had grown quieter and quieter; even Caroline's sobs had petered out to silence, a once-rushing river drying up in a salt flat. The next morning, no one had emerged from their tent, and they'd spent the day grieving for Stephen, for Caroline, for all of those lost, for all they still had to lose.

He heard a rustling outside his tent.

"Adam?"

"In here," he said.

The tent flap drew back and Sarah eased inside. Even by the weak light of the lantern, he could see the sadness etched on her lovely face.

"Have a seat," Adam said, motioning toward the ground.

Sarah took a seat, cross-legged, directly across from Adam.

"Drink?" he said, tilting the bottle toward her.

She shook her head.

"Suit yourself."

He tilted the bottle back and took a drink. The slug went down the wrong way, and he began hacking and coughing, the alcohol burning his nostrils and throat, until he was able to clear his airway.

"You OK?"

He nodded, turning his head and spitting in the corner of the tent. Then he screwed the cap back on the bottle and tossed it near his pillow.

"Sorry."

"I've seen worse."

"You're not here to tell me that I did everything I could, right?"

"Nope. Any idea how he caught it?"

"From his mother, I suppose," he said. "If I had to guess, her antibodies protected him *in utero*, but after he was born, he was on his own."

"That doesn't bode well for us," Sarah said.

"No, it doesn't."

He reached into his bag and took out two chocolate bars.

"Want one?"

"No, thank you."

"You're really turning down a lot of southern hospitality here."

He opened the first bar, snapped off a quarter of it, and popped it in his mouth. He chewed slowly, trying to enjoy the taste, but with the residue of the scotch lingering on his tongue, it tasted bitter and hot.

"You need something?" he asked.

"No need to get nasty."

He rubbed his eyes with the thumb and index finger of his left hand.

"You're right. I'm sorry."

"I thought we needed to talk," she said.

Great, he thought. A big, heaping spoonful of humiliation on top of the shit sundae.

"Nothing to talk about," he said. "I'm a big boy."

"No, I know. You don't understand."

He was too tired to argue, so he sat silently as Sarah struggled to organize her thoughts. He took another bite of the candy bar. This piece tasted a little better.

"It's just that..."

*Chew, chew, chew.*

He honestly had no clue where she was headed, and he figured he could only make things worse by saying anything, so he continued eating the candy bar. When he finished it, he unwrapped the second one.

This seemed to derail her, and she pointed at the chocolate in his hand.

"Really throwing caution to the wind, huh?"

"All that time, worrying about what I ate," he said. "I could be dead tomorrow. Not in the abstract sense, like people used to say. For real. Any of us could be dead tomorrow. After that thing with the fox, I'm lucky I'm not already dead. So I'm going to have two candy bars tonight. And if I'm still alive tomorrow night, I'll have two more."

Then he nodded his head at her, forcefully, demonstrably.

And that was when she started laughing. Her whole body shook, and she clapped her hand over her mouth, presumably to keep herself from making too much noise, but she couldn't stop; the giggles overwhelmed her. Tears streamed down her cheeks, but these weren't tears of sadness. Her eyes sparkled in the dim light, and for a moment, even Adam's chocolate bar tasted good.

The laughter subsided after a few seconds, and then they were back in the moment. She took a few deep breaths to settle herself down.

"The way you nodded your head at me," she said. She pressed the tip of her thumb against her teeth and closed her eyes tight. "That was just too much.

"If you're willing to share," she said, "I think I will take you up on a little of that chocolate."

He snapped off the piece he'd bitten from and handed her the rest. She took a bite and smiled, perhaps tasting the chocolate the way it was supposed to taste, the cocoa hitting her dopamine receptors. He winked at her as he chewed, and she winked back.

"So," Adam said, crumpling up the wrapper and tucking it into his duffel bag. "What was it you wanted to talk about?"

She held the remaining chocolate up.

"You know what?"

He raised his eyebrows.

"I think it can-"

A deep, primal howl exploded through the camp, shattering the night calm. Sarah dropped the candy bar as she scampered to her feet. She pulled the flap of the tent back just enough to peek out toward the center of the camp. Her heart thudded crazily, and she was relieved she'd made it a rule to not go anywhere without her M4. She glanced over at Adam, who'd retrieved his own gun and had taken post opposite her.

Ten seconds.

That's how close she'd come to telling him. Another ten seconds, and she'd have told him about the Huntington's.

*Yeah*, she thought. *Focus on that right now. The camp*

*could be crawling with killers right now, but your near tell-all to the handsome doctor, that's what's important. Idiot.*

She primed her ears and listened for the telltale sounds of intruders in the camp, but she heard nothing. She looked over at Adam, who was craning his head this way and that, trying to make out what was going on, but he shrugged his shoulders upon returning her gaze.

Years of embedded training took over. Yet another drill drilled, another scenario planned for, repeated *ad nauseam* until she could execute it in her sleep. In Iraq and Afghanistan, they gamed it, a terrorist or supposedly friendly local sneaking into camp at night and looking to massacre U.S. soldiers. She ducked out into the darkness, her weapon up and ready, sweeping it from side to side. She scurried along the edge of the tents, trying to stay invisible.

"Help! Somebody help!"

*Freddie.*

Freddie's tent was across the way, but his voice seemed to be coming from this side of the camp, where Caroline had pitched hers. She pulled back the flap of Caroline's tent and ducked inside. The smell was what she noticed first, a thick slap of sourness hanging in the air, as though someone had been sick recently. A lantern glowed in the corner, casting the interior in a ghastly yellow light, the color of sickness and infection and jaundice. Freddie was on his knees in the corner, near Caroline's bedroll, his massive frame blocking Sarah's view of Caroline.

"No, no, no," Freddie was pleading.

"What's wrong?" Adam barked.

"I think she's dead," Freddie said softly, his words coming out in barely a whisper, more like a sigh.

A touch on Sarah's shoulder startled her, and she looked back to see Adam's face, tight and drawn, staring back at her. He had the look of a man who'd seen about all he could take and she glanced away so she wouldn't have to look into that fallen face, that face devoid of anything.

"Let me see," Adam said, curling around Sarah like smoke.

He knelt next to Freddie and felt for a pulse, first in Caroline's wrist and then in her neck. His shoulders sagged, and he rocked back on his haunches, his arms draped over his knees.

"She's dead," Adam said.

Freddie stood up, his head in his hands, grimacing like he was experiencing the world's worst migraine; he paced around the tent, muttering to himself over and over.

"Fuck, fuck, fuck!"

Sarah edged toward Adam for a closer look and saw Caroline's face. Her eyes were open, blank. Her mouth hung open, a thin film on her lips.

"What happened?" Adam asked.

"Couldn't sleep," Freddie said. "Saw her lantern was on so I came over to check on her. Found her lying here."

Adam began scouring Caroline's sleeping area while Freddie resumed his pacing.

"God dammit," Adam muttered a moment later.

"What?" Sarah asked.

He held up a small pill bottle; its amber color glinted in the light of the lantern.

"This is oxycodone," Adam said. "Did anyone know she had these?"

"Oh, no," Freddie said.

"What?"

"She said her leg was bothering her this afternoon and asked me for something," Freddie said.

"Where did you get these?"

"Before we hooked up with you guys. On the road."

"And you didn't think to check with me before prescribing these, Doctor?" Adam snapped.

Freddie stood silently, towering over Sarah and Adam, who looked like a toy action figure next to the big man's mass. Sarah didn't like where this was going at all.

"At least I thought to check on her," Freddie said.

"I'd given her a sleeping pill," Adam said. "I'm her doctor. Not you!"

Freddie's head rocked backward, like a champi-onship boxer taking an unexpected right cross from a lightly regarded challenger. Sarah herself felt her insides drop when she heard this.

"Maybe it was an accident," Sarah offered.

"I specifically told her not to take any other painkillers for this very reason," Adam said.

He stood in the center of the tent with his hands on his hips, shaking his head. Sarah exhaled, sadness rushing in to replace the fear and terror that had gripped her when she'd first heard the scream. She slung her rifle over her shoulder and stared at the sweet woman who now lay dead before her. It had been a shitty couple of months for everyone, but Caroline's surviving Medusa only to watch her first-born perish had seemed particularly cruel.

Death. Death. Death.

It had been a routine part of her adult life, swirling around her like fog. From the first time she'd seen a fellow soldier die in battle, to her first confirmed kill, an insurgent hiding in a house who'd gotten the drop on her only to see his rifle jam, and then blooming into many fellow soldiers and many confirmed kills. She'd expected to die somewhere along the line, not because she was cloaked with an extra-strength dose of bravery in volunteering for the most dangerous missions but because how much better it would have been to die in battle than to be slowly squeezed by Huntington's.

Suicide had never been an option. She could never abandon her troops. As long as she could serve, she couldn't bear the thought of one of her soldiers dying because she hadn't been there for him or her. Even if that meant denying herself an early exit from the scourge that awaited her, the Grim Reaper, his bony arms crossed against his skeletal chest, tapping his foot impatiently. She'd always thought suicide the coward's way out, and even here, she found herself thinking that a little bit about the late Caroline Braddock; she felt bad about thinking it, but that didn't mean she didn't think it.

"I think she left a note," Adam said, derailing Sarah's train of thought.

"It's got your name on it," he said.

Sarah took the page, which had been folded neatly into a square. Sarah's name was etched in big block letters on the outside. She unfolded it and read silently.

*Dear Sarah,*

*I'm sorry for what I've done.*

*But this world fucking sucks. I don't want any part of it. I don't want to live without Stephen. I don't and I won't.*

*Good luck.*

*Love,*

*Caroline*

"What did she say?" Freddie asked.

She tucked the note into her pocket and glanced at Freddie. His eyes were wide with anticipation, and she could see how much it mattered to him to know he'd helped Caroline. She looked at Adam and saw something different, his face blank, his eyes looking somewhere else.

"She said she was sorry. And thank you."

Adam covered Caroline's body with a blanket and extinguished the lantern.

"We can bury her in the morning," he said softly. "It's too dark to do anything now."

They wrapped her body in a blanket, and at first light, Freddie dug a second grave next to Stephen's. Sarah, Nadia and Max watched as Freddie and Adam lowered Caroline into it. They refilled the hole in silence. Sarah was thankful for this; she didn't think she had it in her to hear a rote recitation of platitudes. She'd heard enough eulogies to last ten lifetimes, and at the end of the day, dead was still dead. She had a terrible fear that someone would suggest exhuming Stephen's body so they could bury him with his mother, but mercifully, no one did.

When it was over, they all began packing. No one had to say anything; everyone just seemed to understand it was time to hit the road. They'd been here for nearly two weeks, the longest any of them had spent in one place since the epidemic, but what had once borne the stirrings of home now felt dead and cold. Sarah packed quickly and then helped Max with his things. The baby's death had rattled him badly, and he was morose.

They consulted their maps before pushing out.

"We should head south out of Salina," Adam said, tapping a finger in the center of Kansas. "If we stay on I-70, we could hit snow in the Rockies. We can pick up I-40 in Oklahoma City and turn west there. That will take us south of the mountains."

Sarah found herself nodding in agreement. She sensed a decisiveness in Adam's voice, one that hadn't been there before. She sensed the same thing in the commanding officers she'd looked up to in her career, the ones who'd earned their ranks.

They hit the road in a cool drizzle, and wasn't that the most symbolic thing ever, she thought as the wipers squeaked back and forth across the thick glass. They took I-135 south out of Salina and set a course for Wichita, where they could slingshot around the city onto I-35 and chart a westerly course.

No one spoke.

## 15

I t was the hardest stretch on the road yet. Ninety miles from Salina to Wichita and they'd be walking nearly all of it through an astonishing automobile graveyard. It seemed that as the world had come tumbling down, the residents of each of those cities had concluded that the grass was much greener and healthier in the other. And so into their cars they'd climbed, sick, blind with panic, and in their cars they had died, along that stretch of interstate highway.

A few miles of clear road and then nothing but gridlock. Worse, the traffic jam appeared to be as wide as it was long, spreading off-road into the plains, into the grasslands, creating a sea of steel. Hundreds of thousands of vehicles glinted in the morning light, the shimmer of windshields stretching away to all horizons. They'd tried going around the jam, taking advantage of the big SUV's four-wheel drive, but after a few miles bouncing through thick grasses with no end in sight, they'd abandoned the truck on October 1. But for a short dogleg about halfway between the two cities, the highway ran straight as an arrow. And it was along that long ribbon of asphalt that Adam and the others trekked for those ten days in October.

They averaged eight to ten miles a day through the Big Jam, as they'd taken to calling it. The cars were jammed together like sardines, leaving the narrowest of openings to negotiate. In some places, they'd had to walk topside, skittering from trunk to roof to hood and then back to trunk. And in almost every car, a sad story. A body or three or six. Families. Children. Mommies and Daddies and Nanas and Papas, entombed for all eternity. The bodies dried up and brown.

They made camp early on the seventh day, agreeing that they could use some extra rest, some extra time just doing nothing. As had been their habit, they scoured the vehicles for supplies first and then pitched their tents wherever they could find enough room. The cars were treasure troves of supplies. People had packed well for their final road trips - protein bars and bottled water and medicines, as though any of that could've stopped Medusa's relentless march across the globe.

When they were settled in, Freddie walked the perimeter while the others sat around the campfire. It would be a chilly night, and Adam made a note they'd need to stop for more cold-weather gear when they made it to Wichita. God knew how long they'd be walking. Just a few feet clear of the fire's reach and the night cold gripped hard. Amazing, he thought, the logistics involved in this trek. How their forefathers had done it, without SUVs and Gore-Tex and reliable guns, he'd never know. Just cut from different cloth, he suspected. Tougher cloth.

Max sat across from Adam, the boy's face blank as he scarfed down his dinner. Adam smiled as he watched the boy eat; Max was possessed of a teenage appetite that would not be denied, apocalypse or not. Throw in the long hike they were on, and his stomach was basically a bottomless pit. He was doing reasonably well, Adam thought, given the circumstances. He'd taken a shine to Freddie, that was for sure. Freddie was big, larger than life. Adam still didn't know what the man had done for a living, but it no longer seemed appropriate to ask. That was all in the *Time Before*, when things like that might have mattered. But now they were all the same.

Sarah was making decent progress with Nadia. She was originally from Stillwater and had just turned forty-one a few weeks before the outbreak. Her husband and three teenaged sons had died on four consecutive days in August. That was as far as they'd gotten, but Adam was still impressed. Nadia slept close to Sarah, almost like a frightened child curled up with her mother, and she rarely, if ever, let her out of her sight.

But tonight, she'd had a bit of a breakthrough.

When Adam had served her the canned spaghetti, warmed over the fire, she smiled demurely and said thank you. Those were the first words she had spoken to anyone other than Sarah. It was a small victory, almost nothing, but it had made Adam feel good, an emotion in increasingly short supply. Man, he was beat. It was getting to the point he couldn't remember a world before the epidemic, a world in which he wasn't on this westward quest, his own personal manifest destiny. Sometimes he felt like he'd been on this journey his whole life, that it had no beginning, that it would have no end. A hamster on a wheel.

He reached into his pack for the photograph of Rachel he'd snatched from his bedside stand before leaving Richmond. At first, he'd felt silly taking it. But he was glad he did; he looked at it every night before retiring and every morning before setting off to remind him what was at stake, to keep his eyes on the prize. She was out there somewhere. She had to be. She had to be. He traced the outline of her face with his finger, then along the thick mane of her perpetually messy brown hair. Her eyes were deep brown, like pools of dark chocolate.

He looked up and saw Nadia staring at him, another smile on her face.

"Your family?" she asked. Her voice had a hint of a Texas twang, buried just under the still pronounced Middle Eastern accent.

"I'm sorry?" he said.

"The photograph," she said, nodding toward the picture in Adam's hand.

"Oh," he said. "Yes. My daughter. It's possible she survived."

Nadia's eyes widened at this.

"Really? That would be very unusual, no?"

"Yes. Very. And I'm not one hundred percent certain she's alive. But I have to be sure."

"Of course," Nadia said. "May I?"

Adam proudly handed over the photograph of his daughter, excited to introduce her to someone else. It was times like these he wished he hadn't missed so much of Rachel's childhood, missed the chance to brag about her.

Nadia looked at the photograph and gasped, her hand clapping hard against her mouth. She mumbled something unintelligible, possibly in Arabic. Sarah, who'd been reading by the campfire, looked up, alarm evident on her face.

"Nadia, what's wrong?"

"*Ya Allah, ya Allah, ya Allah,*" she said over and over, staring at the photograph, as though she'd seen a ghost.

"What did you say?" Sarah barked at Adam.

"Nothing! She asked to look at the picture."

"Nadia, what is it?" Sarah said, grabbing Nadia's chin with her hand. Nadia reared back and looked up at Adam, her eyes boring directly into his.

"I know her," Nadia said, pointing at the photograph.

Adam felt his insides drop.

"What do you mean you know her?" Sarah asked.

"She was there. She was there. Rachel."

"Yes, yes!" Adam shouted. "Her name is Rachel."

Adam got up and stumbled around the camp, feeling light-headed, dizzy, almost drunk.

"She's alive?" he said to no one, his hands clasped together behind his head.

Nadia nodded and shifted away from Adam. Maybe he'd freaked her out a little. But Adam didn't care. Tears stung his eyes.

Rachel was alive. Rachel was alive. His daughter was alive.

"YEAAAAAAAAAHHHHHHHHH!" he howled, his bellow echoing across the empty plains like a sonic wave.

～

Sleep was hard to come by that night. All Adam could think about was Rachel. Out there in the cold, in the dark, in a world that had fallen, Rachel lived on.

He would find her if it was the last thing he did.

TO BE CONTINUED IN...




EVERGREEN

THE IMMUNE - BOOK 3

## PREVIEW OF EVERGREEN

Stupidity.

Sheer, unvarnished, in-the-raw stupidity. Free-range, organic stupidity.

That's what had gotten her in this mess.

Rattled by the horror that had unfolded before her, she had made decisions she never would have made in ordinary circumstances, and that's what really pissed her off - with her back against the wall, she'd failed to make the right decisions at the moments they'd mattered most. You'd never have busted Rachel Fisher for something asinine like going to the grocery store on an empty stomach, but, no, no, when the apocalypse hits, she'd run around like a goddamn fool. She'd done what *other* people did, people who let their emotions get the best of them, heat-of-passion decisions.

Perhaps it could be excused, and maybe someone else would've been quicker to forgive herself.

But not Rachel Fisher.

And now here she was, stirring her bubbling pot of regret like a thick soup in winter.

Now that she was here, she was trying to keep her wits about her. Focus. Study. Learn. The others were panicky, weepy. But Rachel didn't want to be like the others. She wanted to know more about this place, find out what the hell was going on. They'd started to look to her, these women that were ten or fifteen years her senior, looking to her for answers, for reassurance, for help. She didn't know why. She'd never been particularly good at making friends, and she really hadn't had many in her life. It wasn't that she didn't want friends, it was just that she seemed to be missing some key piece of equipment that let people connect with one another in some meaningful way.

She was lying on her side, dressed in the sky-blue jumpsuit that was their standard uniform. She studied her arm, the small $\pi$ etched on the inside of her left wrist. It was weird to look at the tat now, this thing she'd carried with her from the old world; in fact, it was the only thing she had left from before. Never had she thought she'd have a tattoo, but it was math, and she was a programmer, and that made it seem okay. On the opposite wrist, of course, was the tattoo these monsters had tagged her with, but she didn't bother looking at that one anymore.

The room was small and getting smaller each day, a noose tightening around her, threatening to choke off her sanity. A cot. A small banker's box, in which she kept her three jumpsuits and the few personal effects the captives were allowed. She got up and crossed over to the window, a perk of the room for which she was ever grateful. The prairie stretched on interminably, stark and endless. She thought they were in Kansas or Nebraska, but she wasn't entirely sure about that. The last few days had been relatively uneventful. No testing, no speeches or ridiculous orientation sessions. Just three relatively square meals and an hour of free time in the yard with her fellow captives.

Rachel didn't know who these people were, but there was something very off about them. Granted, she'd been a loner most of her life, happiest in the soft glow of a computer screen or with a problem set. She wasn't good at small talk, and she was even worse at big talk, and so as she'd gotten older, she'd become more and more comfortable with herself and less comfortable with the world outside her door. But when she thought about the dead world around her, the panic would rise up like a rapidly inflating balloon, taking her breath away. These people, however, seemed to have taken the end of the world in stride.

Just because she didn't play nicely with others didn't mean she'd welcomed mankind's extermination, and she would think about math and programming and remind herself that unchecked emotion wasn't going to help anything, certainly not how to solve the mess she was in. And now she thought back to her life, and how she'd spent most of her years avoiding other people. One evening, a couple of weeks before the outbreak, she'd been at a Starbucks with her laptop; a nice guy wearing those tight jeans had started chatting with her, and she had just ignored him, trying to disappear into the glow of her MacBook. Why did she do things like that? And now, she supposed, that nice guy was almost certainly dead.

Jesus, what a cluster-fuck the end of the world had turned out to be.

She'd been getting ready to head back to CalTech when the virus hit Southern California like a meteor. By August 15, commercial air travel had been shut down, the buses and trains had stopped running, hell, all interstate travel had been banned, and it hadn't made a lick of difference. Medusa still got in, the most uninvited guest of all time, and burned through the population like a brushfire.

Her stepdad Jerry had gone totally ape-shit when things started to get bad. He'd barricaded them in the house, filled the tub with water, rationed out the food. She'd argued with him, telling him he was blowing things out of proportion (and if she was being honest with herself now, she was worried he'd mess up her upcoming move back to Pasadena). He didn't sleep, spent every waking minute in front of the television, his iPad and iPhone close by, Twitter feeds monitored. Internet access became spotty around August 15, but by then, it was spitting out the same old shit hour after hour after hour.

None of them got sick until the sixteenth, when her mom woke up with it, crying. Jerry had quarantined her in her bedroom, leaving food and water at the door, and that hadn't gone over particularly well, especially after Jerry came down with it. At first, and she was ashamed to admit it to herself, even now, two months after it had happened, she'd been fascinated by the outbreak, to be alive for such a paradigm shift. But then her mom had died on August 17, and Jerry was dead by the eighteenth. Although she hadn't been that close to her mom and Jerry was kind of an idiot, watching them die had been pretty goddamn horrible because she saw how she would die. But then a day would go by, then another, and then another, and it began to dawn on her that she wasn't going to catch it.

Then the urge to see another living person, any living person, became overwhelming, and she finally was ready to chance going outside. On the afternoon of the nineteenth, she tiptoed down the brick walk with a kitchen knife in hand, the sun shining the sky crystal clear blue, so blue it made your head hurt. And far away, she'd hear a wayward gunshot or a mournful scream, like she was hearing a television in another room. House by house in their tony subdivision she had gone, knocking on doors, looking for someone, anyone who was still alive, and every door remained pulled tight. Six doors down, her knocks had been greeted by a series of painful moans, which had scared her back down the porch steps and fleeing for the safety of her bedroom, her bladder letting go on the way back. Still wearing her soiled clothes, she hid under the bed the rest of that day and all that night, like Macauley Culkin in *Home Alone*.

By August 20, when the sirens and helicopters buzzing overhead were gone and the power was out and the silence encased the city in a thick crust, she decided it was time to take action. With her mom and Jerry lying dead in their bedroom, because she didn't know what the hell to do with their bodies, she sat at their expensive antique dining table and made a list of *Things to Do*. It was a project, one she nicknamed *Shawshank*, a little homage to her mom's favorite movie, the one with Tim Robbins spending two decades in a Maine prison for a double murder he didn't commit. It was not unlike the programming projects or computer hacks she'd undertaken. You start with a goal, and you just worked backward from the end result you wanted and then figured out the pieces you absolutely had to have to get to that outcome.

Tahoe had been a bust. She'd made it to the outskirts of town on August 28, only to find it had burned to the ground, nothing left but smoldering ruins, thick tendrils of smoke still reaching for the sky. With that gone and done with, she decided to head east, holding out hope her dad was still alive. It sounded like he'd survived deep into the second week, and well, it wasn't like she had many other options. The idea that he was still alive was grist for the mill, enough to keep her moving each day, especially as the scope of the disaster became apparent. So she had headed east, back toward the place she'd been born, for the first time since her mom had moved her out to California nearly two decades earlier.

By mid-September, she'd made it east of the Rockies, past Denver, feeling pretty good about herself. And then she'd gone and gotten herself caught by these yahoos.

At precisely seven a.m., the jiggle of the door, which, of course, only locked from the outside. She leapt out of bed to greet her guard, Ned. He was a tall, nervous fellow with a narrow face that he was constantly touching with his slender fingers. As captors went, he was about as good as one could hope for. He was almost apologetic about it. He rarely spoke and refused to make eye contact, as though he was embarrassed to be part of this.

"Good morning, Ned," she said, as warmly and

cheerily as she could. The greeting had become part of their daily dance, and per their usual agreement, Ned replied with an almost imperceptible nod.

"You just don't seem like the kind of guy to get caught up in all this," she said.

Each day, she'd dug a little deeper, a little at a time. She didn't know where any of this was going, but it was a project that might one day bear fruit. An experiment you stuck in the corner of the lab and maybe it paid dividends down the road.

He let out a small sigh, one he may not have intended, and he caught himself midstream. He looked at her for a moment, scrunching up his lips as though he were deep in thought. Even though they were alone in the room, he glanced over his shoulder.

"What's it really like out there?" he whispered.

Her eyes went wide.

"Don't you know?"

"Management keeps things kind of close to the vest."

"It was bad, Ned."

She let that set for a moment before continuing.

"Every city and town in America is a rotting, stinking graveyard. It killed almost everybody."

She paused for dramatic effect and then repeated the last word slowly, emphasizing each syllable.

"Now I want to ask you a question," she said, moving in while his guard was down, while he was processing her report from the field. "What am I doing here?"

His eyes, which had been drifting, snapped into focus.

"We shouldn't be talking about this," he whispered.

Rachel's heart leapt into her throat. Not a *shut up*, but the more conspiratorial *we shouldn't*.

"Bad enough what your bosses are doing," she said. Important to start separating him from the monsters at the top. "It has to stop."

"Stop it," he snapped at her.

Enough, she told herself. That was enough for today. But the plant was starting to bear fruit, if only a small bud. A healthy bud, perhaps, but still a small bud. Too much attention now could strangle it.

They ate breakfast together every morning, to the extent it could be called breakfast. They ate protein bars and MREs. Vitamins. Water. Coffee, but shit coffee, like someone had re-brewed it through a used diaper. Part of her was surprised that they let the women commingle like sorority sisters at brunch, but she gathered it was important to their captors that they enjoy a semblance of normalcy.

After breakfast was their hour in the yard. A six-foot-high fence had been strung around their building, leaving them just a little patch of hardpack to get all the fresh air they were going to get for the day. Rachel chose to walk the perimeter, ever mindful of the guards with their automatic weapons. The complex was unlike any place she'd ever seen. Fortress like. Off in the distance, to her west and north, high walls enclosed the compound.

Sounds of activity elsewhere in the compound filled the air. Generators, trucks, tractors, revving to life on this cool but not cold morning. Life was moving on here, and for the thousandth time, she wished she knew more about this place. So many questions.

Who were these people?

What were they doing here?

Had anyone died of the plague here?

Had they really just ridden it out?

And most importantly: What was in store for her and the other women?

She'd made a full loop of the perimeter when she noticed a handful of women had gathered at the center of the yard.

This was the crying group, the ones committed to telling their sad stories of the plague over and over, in new and horrifying ways. And they were at it again this morning. Stories of how this child or that spouse had died, when they had died, what they had done after the person had died. Why relive it? She tried to listen and understand it from their point of view. Maybe the simple act of telling it flushed it out, leached the poison from their systems. The fact that all of them had experienced the same kinds of losses, she supposed, didn't make each person's individual loss any less profound. She had to remember that. Her mom had died, but she'd known lots of people who'd lost a parent and it hadn't been the end of the world (*except in her case, it had been, ha-ha, will this gallows humor ever STOP?*), and her dad might even still be alive, so who was she to judge them and their terrible fate?

Was it because she was still single and childless?

Was she just a sociopath?

Erin Thompson was telling her tale now, the tears flowing, her shoulders heaving. Rachel looked at her, she really looked at her. She was a pretty woman, down there deep, underneath the grief, underneath the hard shell that had formed in the years she had spent constructing her appropriate middle-class life. It no longer mattered whether it had made her happy or whether she had mortgaged her dreams to become a stay-at-home mom because all of it, from the endless parade of birthday parties to her husband's somewhat lackadaisical attitude toward marriage and fatherhood and family in general, was better than this hellscape in which they'd been abandoned.

"All my life, I prayed to God to protect my family," she said. Then: "God can go fuck Himself!"

A few of the other women gasped, and two crossed themselves. Undone. These women were coming undone, a little bit at a time.

She glanced around the faces that grew more familiar every day. One of the faces that had been there in the early days was still missing. The Middle Eastern woman, Nadia. A sweet lady. This would be the third or fourth day that Rachel hadn't seen her. Maybe she'd escaped. She was probably dead.

So easy, that word. Dead. Once spoken in hushed tones, never around children unless it was spelled out, and always with eternal respect, lest it be your lot sooner than later, now it was just a word. A market flooded with it, its value cheapened.

But that was the thing. While dead might have become valueless currency, life was now the gold standard. Simply by being alive, Nadia had earned some measure of respect. Undoubtedly, her very existence had been important to these people.

But why?

As sex slaves?

Given the number of female faces she'd seen, many of them quite attractive, that didn't quite add up. Dozens of beautiful women here, lean, athletic, vibrant, intelligent. And Rachel's group of twelve was, on the surface, very ordinary. She herself didn't hold a candle to most of the women here. This wasn't low self-esteem talking; it was just who she was. After a classmate's messy death from anorexia in high school, Rachel had long since made her peace with her slightly pear-shaped build.

And just like that, the hour was up, and Ned and the other guard herded them back inside. Rachel took in a lungful of fresh air, fixating on its cool sweetness, something to remember as she spent the next twenty-three hours indoors. Ned escorted her again, his face looking long and drawn. He kept looking at her, long enough for her to catch him, and then he would cut his eyes away. She wondered if she could trade what she knew about the outside for more information about what was happening here.

As they made their way down the narrow corridor back to her room, the last one on the end, she considered faking a sexual interest in him, but she dismissed the idea just as quickly. For one thing, she'd never tried anything like that before, and she didn't think she was a good enough actor to pull it off. But the most important reason was that she sensed she had the upper hand in the relationship. As a woman, she'd been a relative rarity in her chosen field. Something like ninety percent of engineers and programmers had been men, and she'd drawn her share of interest at CalTech and during her two summer internships. Even from the gross professors, who'd had years to perfect their game with the undergraduates, but still pathetic with their clumsy, one-beat-too-long invites for a programming session and "hey let's order some Chinese food and I've got this bottle of wine someone left in my office," like they were reading from a script of a romantic comedy making fun of dirty old computer geeks.

"You lose anyone?" she asked as they arrived at her room. All the other women were secured in their rooms.

"No," he said harshly.

He shoved her into her room. As he stepped back out into the hallway, he paused and looked back over his shoulder.

"My sister and her family," he whispered. "They lived outside Chicago. I don't know what happened to them."

"I'm sorry," she said.

He scraped a flake of dried paint from the doorjamb.

"Sometimes things are different in practice than in theory," he said.

"What?"

"Nothing. I'll be back at dinner," he said.

He walked away without another word.

# ABOUT THE AUTHOR

David's first novel, *The Jackpot*, was a No.1 bestselling legal thriller. He is also the author of *The Immune*, *The Living*, *Anomaly*, and *The Nothing Men*.

His short comedy films about law and publishing have amassed more than 2.5 million hits on YouTube and have been featured on CNN, in *The Washington Post*, *The Huffington Post*, and *The Wall Street Journal*.

Visit him at his website or follow him on Facebook (David Kazzie, Author) and Twitter (@davidkazzie).

Made in the USA
Monee, IL
21 July 2020